WE'RE AT THE OLD HEADSTONE.

JFC

Suddenly there's an inexplicable smile on my face. My heart feels warm and safe despite my body being pummeled by rain and wind. I wonder if this is what it's like to have two parents. If having two parents always makes your heart feel warm.

It doesn't matter if it's not his headstone. It doesn't matter if this isn't actually where he's buried. My dad has been hanging out here, at this headstone with his initials, as close to me as he could be.

The wind dies down and it feels like his arms are around my shoulders as I kneel there in the grass.

"I can't believe I have to leave without the answer," I say out loud. Then I open the earth to bury the last question I'll ever bury in this graveyard.

Will you forgive me if I never find you?

ALSO BY CAELA CARTER

My Life with the Liars
Forever, or a Long, Long Time
How to Be a Girl in the World

caela carter

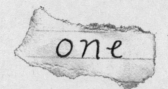

one

speck

of

truth

HARPER
An Imprint of HarperCollinsPublishers

Library of Congress Cataloging-in-Publication Data

Names: Carter, Caela, author.
Title: One speck of truth / Caela Carter.
Description: First edition. | New York, NY : Harper, an imprint of HarperCollins
    Publishers, [2019] | Summary: "Alma yearns for the truth about her dead
    birth father, and a trip to his birthplace might provide the answers she
    desperately seeks"-- Provided by publisher.
Identifiers: LCCN 2018025429 | ISBN 978-0-06-267268-1 (paperback)
Subjects: | CYAC: Mothers and daughters--Fiction. | Secrets--Fiction. | Fathers and
    daughters--Fiction. | Identity--Fiction. | BISAC: JUVENILE FICTION / Social
    Issues / Emotions & Feelings. | JUVENILE FICTION / Family / Parents. |
    JUVENILE FICTION / People & Places / Europe.
Classification: LCC PZ7.C24273 One 2019 | DDC [Fic]--dc23 LC record
    available at https://lccn.loc.gov/2018025429

Typography by Erin Fitzsimmons
20 21 22 23 24   PC/BRR   10 9 8 7 6 5 4 3 2 1
❖
First paperback edition, 2020

For Melissa

one

A HISTORY OF QUESTIONS

WHEN I WAS FOUR, I ASKED my mom a question. Eight years later I'm still waiting for the answer.

I was sitting on my mom's lap at our new kitchen table in our new tiny apartment, just the two of us, no Nanny and PopPop. We were sharing a dinner out of cardboard take-out boxes.

"Mom," I said. "Where's my dad?"

I felt my mom's legs stiffen underneath mine. She cleared her throat. "You heard what Nanny said. He passed away."

"I know," I said. "But where is he? Nanny said he's in a graveyard."

"Yes," my mom said.

"But where is the graveyard?"

Mom didn't say anything else. She took a bite of her food. She shifted.

"Did you read any books at school today?" she asked.

"Where is the graveyard?" I said.

"I'll tell you when you're older," Mom said. "Did you read any books at school today?"

"How old?" I asked. "Seven?"

"I don't know, Alma," Mom said, her voice getting louder.

"Twelve?" I asked. Back then, twelve seemed very old.

"Alma. Enough. We are changing the subject."

And she was the grown-up and I was the kid. So when she spoke hard and loud like that, all the thoughts swimming around in my brain stopped mattering. Or at least they seemed not to matter. Or at least they seemed not to matter to anyone else. They were mine, of course, the questions. So they've always mattered to me.

When I was six, I tried it a little differently.

We were sitting at our new-new kitchen table in our new-new house all the way out in Pennsylvania, far from Nanny and PopPop in Florida.

I sat across from my mom, rearranging the meatballs on top of my spaghetti.

I didn't look at her. I thought maybe if I didn't look at her, I could trick her into answering.

"So is the right graveyard near where we are now? Because now we live close to where you grew up. Or maybe it's near where Nanny and PopPop live? Because that's where we lived when I was as a baby."

Mom coughed as if a piece of meatball were stuck in her

throat. I still didn't look at her.

"Or is it all the way in Portugal?"

I didn't want to see the way she narrowed her gray eyes when I asked a question. I didn't want to see the way her bun was wound tight, tight, tighter on the back of her head. I didn't want to see her perfect posture. All the ways she was better than me.

"The *right* graveyard?" she finally said, like the words were from some nonsense language. "What do you mean by 'right graveyard'?"

But I knew she knew what I meant.

I speared a meatball with my fork and to it I said, "The one where my dad—"

"Alma," Mom interrupted. She sighed. "Not today. I'm tired."

I bit my lip, embarrassed and angry. But also a little determined. I'd find out where he was, even if she didn't want me to.

"Be a good girl and stop asking questions," Mom said.

But if good girls were girls with no questions, I wasn't a good girl. I couldn't be.

I was determined to find him so I decided to ask every day. Every day she would say no, she wouldn't tell me.

She said the same thing for so many days in a row that I finally called Nanny and asked her.

"He's near you, sweetheart. Of course he's near where you live now."

When I tried to ask more questions, Nanny cut me off just like Mom did. "Some answers need to wait until you're older."

By the time I was eight, I had found him. But that didn't chase all the questions away.

"Where did you meet?" I asked Mom one night.

"We met in Lisbon. In Portugal," she said. "When I was spending my junior year of college abroad. You know that."

"Yeah," I said. "But where in Lisbon?"

Mom turned her back to me. She was cooking. I was alone at the kitchen table this time.

"I don't remember all the details, Alma," Mom said. She sounded tired. I made her tired.

"You got married, right?" I said.

Mom said nothing. She rearranged pans on the stove, then walked to the counter next to it and put her elbows down so her back was pointing toward me.

"You were in love, right?"

She put her head in her hands right there on the counter.

"What did he say when I was born?" I asked. "Did he look like me?"

Mom rubbed her forehead.

"Did he want me to have his last name?"

"*Enough*, Alma," Mom said. She was always sick of the questions. I couldn't stop them from coming. I didn't know how. And, sometimes, I didn't want to anyway.

"Enough," she said again. Even though I had stopped. For now.

Enough. That was the only answer I got.

When I was ten, Mom and Adam were married. I tried to ask him instead.

"Do I have any family still in Portugal?" I asked.

He was driving me to a piano lesson. So I didn't have to look at him, but also he couldn't run away.

"You'll have to ask your mother, Alma," Adam said.

"Did you know my dad is buried in the graveyard behind the McKinleys' house?"

Adam raised his eyebrows and looked at me in the rear-view mirror. "You'll have to ask your mother about that," he said.

"Did he love me?" I asked.

Adam didn't answer for a minute. He pulled the car over and turned around so he could look at me.

"Alma. Of course he loved you," Adam whispered. "You're the most lovable kid in the world."

"Oh," I said.

I took that answer and tucked it into a pocket right in the middle of my heart. He loved me. My dad loved me.

The rest of the questions were still humming in my brain, but they quieted a little with that one answer.

He loved me.

Later, I asked my mom that question.

I guess that was a good question for some reason because she actually answered it.

"Of course," she said. "Of course he loved you."

But she didn't look up from her work to say it.

A few weeks ago, when I was newly twelve, I found my mom on the little couch in the living room, surrounded by papers, her glasses pushed up on her head.

Her eyes were red and there was a tissue next to her so I knew she'd been crying, even though she always tries to hide her sadness from me.

Sadness and questions belong in other people's houses. Not ours.

I asked a question anyway, of course.

I asked a new kind of question.

"Mom," I said. "Where's Adam?"

"Alma," she said like I'd done something wrong. Like I'd thrown a ball through the window or put already-chewed gum under the couch cushions. "I swear, if you don't ask me another question for a hundred years it'll be too soon."

It was like she slapped me.

She slapped me with her words.

So now I have new questions.

A pile of new questions.

A heap of new questions.

And they are piling, heaping on top of the mountain of my old questions.

I used to be a girl but I'm not anymore.

Questions are my bones, my blood, my organs.

I've been overtaken by questions.

I can't ask my mom anymore.

Instead, I find a way to ask my dad.

two
WHERE'S ADAM?

MY BEST FRIEND, JULIA, DOESN'T KNOW about the No Questions Rule. Julia lives in a normal family with normal rules. Julia is an actual good girl who doesn't ask the questions she isn't supposed to.

Julia, Mom, and I are sitting at our kitchen table with cartons of Chinese food open between the three of us. Julia and I have spent almost every minute of this summer before sixth grade together. But she hasn't been here in weeks. It's better when we sleep over at her house.

"Hey," she says.

My heart speeds up. I know what she's going to say before her mouth opens. She's going to ask a question.

Not the sort of safe question that Mom allows, like "Can I have more milk?" or "Is there still a TV in the living room so we can watch a movie?"

She's going to ask a Bad Girl Question. She won't know it's a Bad Girl Question because I haven't told her or anyone what's been happening in my house.

"Hey," she says again. "Where's Uncle Adam?"

A piece of stir-fried broccoli lodges in my throat and I cough.

If I were the one asking, Mom would say, "Don't ask me that right now, Alma."

Or "The details are not for the children to know."

Or "Go practice the piano."

But Mom doesn't say anything to Julia. She gets up and pours me a glass of water. My face burns as I take a sip.

Finally she says, "That's actually private family business."

Julia looks stunned.

I feel stunned. If it's private family business, I must not be part of the family. No one has explained to me where my stepdad—or maybe ex-stepdad—is now that he's not here anymore. A few weeks ago I saw him putting a suitcase in his car. "Alma," he said. "You know my number. You call me when it gets really bad."

I didn't know what that meant but he didn't give me time to ask. He squashed me into a hug, then rushed into his car and drove away.

Since then, Mom hasn't told me anything. Nothing. Zilch.

But I'm pretty sure he's gone forever.

Julia's looking at her shoes. She's embarrassed like I am.

Mom is good at that.

Reminding us how small we are.

Reminding us how little we need to know.

Mom comes into my room at ten on the dot. Julia is sprawled out on her sleeping bag on my rug, braiding a friendship bracelet. I'm sitting at my desk, surrounded by scraps of loose-leaf paper. On each I write one sentence.

One question.

What would you have said to me on my birthday this year?

Where did you and my mom like to go to have fun?

How old were you when you died?

As soon as I see my mom, I scramble to gather all the scraps of paper, hiding them in my hands. She can't know about the questions. They belong to only me. Until I can give them to my dad.

"Lights out, girls," Mom says.

At Julia's house we don't have a Lights-Out time during sleepovers.

"I have to brush my teeth!" Julia says, jumping to her feet. Mom sighs.

I stand to pull back my covers and get into my bed. Mom is staring at me. Her bun is so tight it makes the skin stretch thin on her forehead.

"I already brushed mine," I say.

"Lights-out is at ten," Mom says, as if it's my fault Julia didn't brush her teeth yet.

Lights-out used to be at ten for me and ten thirty for Mom. But recently I've seen the light on under her door late into the night. Mom is forgetting her own rules half the time, but she doesn't forget mine ever.

Julia comes back and crawls into her sleeping bag.

Mom crosses the room and plants a kiss on my forehead. "I love you, Alma. I do everything I do just for you."

She says the same thing every night. She likes it when one day looks exactly like the day before. It's my favorite part of her everyday same things. Hearing that she loved me that day. No matter what Bad Questions I accidentally asked. No matter what I forgot to do or did that I shouldn't have done. She always tells me she loves me at the end of the day.

I take my big green glasses off and put them on my night table.

"Good night, girls."

Julia waits until my mom's footsteps have disappeared down the hallway before asking the Bad Question again into the darkness.

"Alma," she whispers. "Where was Uncle Adam tonight?"

I bite my lip. Blood oozes out and into my mouth, metallic and gross and a perfect reminder that I didn't actually brush my teeth.

When I don't answer, Julia wiggles out of her sleeping bag and sits on the edge of my bed. She's blurry next to me.

"Is he gone?" she asks.

I look at her. My breath feels like fire.

"Did they break up?" she asks.

I can't make myself answer. She figures it out though.

"I didn't know," she says. "I don't think he told my dad."

Julia thinks that matters because her dad is Adam's brother.

But I was more than that. I was his kid.

He didn't tell *me*.

"This is awful," Julia says. "I get it. It's awful."

I scoot away from her. Her parents still hold hands across the dinner table. I see them kiss each other every time one of them enters the room. And her parents are alive. She doesn't get it at all.

"He was only my stepfather," I mumble, not looking at her. "I'll get over it."

My breath cools, comes in and out of my mouth smooth and easy. Lying makes me feel better.

"Do you want to talk about it?"

Yes, I think. *Yes, more than anything.*

"I'm fine," I say.

"OK," Julia says slowly, like she doesn't believe me. But she gets off my bed and wiggles into her sleeping bag. It's only minutes before she's snoring.

I watch the clock tick slowly. My room somehow gets darker and darker even though the sun was already down before we went to sleep. Or maybe it's my thoughts getting darker. In the lonely darkness, all I can think about is both of my dads. Both of my missing dads.

At 2:00 a.m. I figure my mom must be asleep.

I get out of bed, put my glasses back on, and slip my flip-flops on. I pull my hoodie on over my pajamas. The right pocket rustles with scraps of questions, the left one is heavy with the tools I need. I tiptoe over Julia's sleeping body, then down the hallway. My mom's door is dark. Perfect.

I go out the back door in the kitchen. It's as easy as it always is. Julia never wakes up. Mom never suspects anything. If I didn't spend so many nights at Julia's, I could do this every night.

The moon is full, lighting up our backyard and glinting, silver, off our wet grass. It feels like it just stopped raining. The world smells fresh and new and, with the trees at the back of our yard spread out before me and the moon round above me, I feel like I'm the only one in it. It's the perfect night for what I'm about to do. I dart through our yard and weave my way through the trees until I'm in the McKinleys' yard. I run around their pool, around their house, and across the gravel road in front of it. I run up the little hill at the other side, jump over the train tracks, run down the little hill. Then I feel along the green wire fence until I find the crack in it, right where it always is. I squeeze through and take a deep breath, exhilarated and calm all at once.

My dad tugs on my heart. My heart had been solidly in place but then it feels like he hooks a finger right in the spot where all four quadrants meet and he yanks it toward him. "Hi," I whisper into the mist around me.

The graveyard is beautiful in the moonlight, the white

headstones seeming to grow out of the blackness around them. The wet grass tickles the sides of my feet.

I walk the ten feet or so until I find his grave.

His headstone is simple. Gray. About the size of four bricks pushed together. Long grass grows on all the sides, covering up all but the surface of it. His initials are carved into the top of it: JFC.

Jorge Francisco Costa.

I think he must have wanted such a simple headstone. I think he must have been humble and reserved.

I think that also must be why he said it was OK for me to have my mom's last name. He was humble. He was a feminist. He was a perfect dad. Or he would have been.

I imagine him sick in a hospital bed, telling my mom what he would want after he was gone. She'd have to lean over her big belly, pregnant with me inside, to listen as he told her in a dying voice what he wants in a tombstone and a funeral. I'd be listening too, inside layers of flesh and amniotic fluid, and I'd hear her tell him, "Yes, OK. Whatever you want, babe."

Because my dad must have made my mom better. Softer. Easier to love.

My dad must have been very loving. Because even with all the Bad Questions, even with all the times I break the rules, he still loves me. Even across the abyss of death, he still loves me.

That's about the only thing Mom has ever told me about him.

That's the one thing I've never questioned.

That's my speck of truth.

He loves me.

I sit to the right of his headstone, next to where his body is under the earth. I reach a hand out and put it on the grass beside me, as if he is lying there sick and I can hold his hand.

We don't talk. We never do. But that's only because he's dead. I know if he were alive he would talk to me constantly.

I sit still long enough that my pajama pants start to get damp from the wet grass. My shoulder starts to ache from reaching my hand out to him. I start to yawn.

I should stay longer. I always think that if I could just make myself stay here a little longer, he would come to me. He would bring me answers. But I'm weak and I get uncomfortable and tired.

I slip the garden spade out of my pocket and make a new hole. The grass in front of his tombstone is pockmarked with little holes where I've left questions in the past. Then I dig in my other pocket. I choose the most important scrap of paper and straighten it out. I open the earth on top of my dad's grave and plant my question above him for him to answer. Then I cover it up using my garden spade. I always try to put the earth and the grass back exactly as I found them so you have to look closely to see the little marks I've left behind. But if you do, you'll know. I don't bring my dead dad flowers and Christmas wreaths like a normal girl.

I bring him questions. I bring him the Bad Questions.

I imagine him reaching his skeleton hand up toward the scrap of paper. I imagine him hooking the bones of what used to be his index finger around it and bringing it down into his casket.

I know he's frustrated.

I know he's crying for me.

I know he would give me the answers if he could.

This one might be the worst question ever. Even worse than Julia's question at dinner.

Did Adam stop loving me?

"Answer this one," I beg him. "Please find a way."

Of course he doesn't say anything. He never does. He can't.

I sit and stare at the spot where I left the question. Then he says my name.

"Alma!"

It's clear as a church bell ringing on a silent Sunday morning. I jump three feet in the air.

"Alma!"

Then I turn. It's not my dad.

It's Julia.

three

WHERE ARE YOU?

JULIA IS JUST INSIDE THE GRAVEYARD fence, walking toward me. She found the crack in it. She must have followed me.

I shove the garden spade into my pocket. How much did she see? How much did the darkness protect me?

Julia tells me everything about her life. And she tells me that she tells me everything. I know all about how lucky she feels to have been adopted from Korea, even if she sometimes doesn't like sticking out in her white family. She tells me all the good and bad things. She says we're best friends and best friends know everything about each other. But I can't even start to think about telling Julia everything about me. There's too much about me that I don't even know.

"Who were you talking to?" Julia asks when she reaches my side.

I'm still sitting in the grass.

"What are you doing here?" I say, looking up at her.

She raises her eyebrows above her square black glasses. "I'm here because you are. What are *you* doing here?"

I bite my lip again. It's still sore in the spot I made bleed earlier.

"I noticed the last time I slept over that you left in the middle of the night. But you didn't tell me about it in the morning. So this time I followed you. What are you doing?"

I bite down harder.

"Please, Alma? Tell me. I'm your best friend."

And she is. Any other friend would run away from someone as weird as me.

"It's my dad," I say. I point to his headstone.

My face is burning and I'm sure it's red but she can't see it in the darkness. I don't want her to ask me how I know. I don't want to have to tell her that I went out here and searched all the graves when I was eight years old, that I read them all over and over again until I found the right one. I don't want her to know that no one ever told me he was here. I don't want her to know how little my family tells me, how little they think of me.

Julia's eyebrows fall. She kneels next to me. "Oh," she says, hushed. "This is his grave?"

"Yes," I say.

She looks at it. "JFC?" she says.

"Jorge Francisco Costa," I say. "That was his name. This must be his grave."

As soon as I say it, I want to eat the words.

"What do you mean, it *must* be?" she asks.

I shrug.

"Did your mom tell you this is where he's buried?"

"She told me he was close by," I say quickly. "Well, Nanny told me that. My grandmother. And this is the closest grave-yard to my house."

Julia stands up and looks at the headstone. She squats next to it and squints. She starts brushing the high grass around the headstone. She's looking so closely I'm a little worried she'll notice all the indentations in the grass.

But she doesn't. She turns back to me with her mouth open and a look on her face that only means she feels sorry for me.

"Alma," she says.

I stand. "No. Don't say what you're going to say. It's his grave. I know it is. It has to be."

"Alma," she says again. "I don't think—"

I cut her off. "Do you know how many nights I've spent out here? This is my dad. It has to be. I feel him here. He squeezes my heart the minute I sneak through the fence. He sits with me here and he tries to answer . . ." I stop. I've said way too much.

Julia deserves a best friend who is fun. Who loves sleepovers in the living room with late-night snacks and mov-ies. I try hard to be that for her. I try hard not to show her the girl who loves to be in graveyards more than anywhere else in the world.

Julia is shaking her head.

"What?" I ask. "Just say it, OK?"

She points to his headstone. "Did you read the rest of this?" she asks. She moves the grass in the front of the headstone to the side.

"The rest of what?" I demand. "It just says JFC. Jorge Francisco Costa."

I'm talking too loudly. So loudly maybe the McKinleys will wake up and hear me and call my mom. I can't help it. My heart is sinking. My knees are weak.

Julia hasn't even explained anything yet and I already know she's right.

But she can't be right.

This has to be him.

"There are dates," she says. "Under the initials. See them? There are dates on the headstone."

"Dates?"

A picture dances in my brain. My dad and my softer mother leaning close across a candlelit table.

"Like the dates he lived. Or she. Whoever this is. JFC."

"He," I say. But quieter. My voice is shaking like the rest of me.

"It says 1901 to 1973," she whispers.

"But . . . but I wasn't born in 1973," I say.

"You weren't even close to born in 1973," she says.

I sink back to my knees and hold the headstone in each of my hands. I see the numbers, carved so small underneath the JFC: 1901–1973. How could I never have noticed that before? How could I be so stupid?

So many things fall away. The idea that my dad is humble and reserved because he only wanted his initials on his headstone. The image of him holding hands with my mom while I listened to his voice through her belly.

All the questions I've ever asked.

No wonder he hasn't given me answers. I've been asking the wrong person.

I look up at Julia. Her eyes are red, almost like she's the one who just lost her dad.

"I'm sorry, Alma," she says. She crouches next to me and puts her arm around me. I let her.

I adjust my glasses and look into her eyes.

"Where is he?" I ask it as if she'll give me an answer. I ask it as if she has all the information my mom has but with the attitude my dad would have if he were still alive.

"You have to ask your mom," she says.

I take a shaky breath. I have to tell her the truth. "I can't," I say. "She won't tell me."

"Oh," Julia says. "OK. I get that."

I hate when she says that. She gets it. She doesn't. She couldn't. Her mom tells her everything.

She takes a deep breath and says, "Then we'll have to find him ourselves."

I forgive her immediately.

"We?" I say.

She nods.

"You'll help?" I ask.

Julia looks around. "I don't like graveyards," she says. "Especially not at night . . . But for you, yes. I'd help you do anything."

I jump and wrap my arms around her. "Thank you! Thank you!" I say.

"Just like you'd help me, right?" she says.

"Right!" I say. "Promise!"

It's an easy promise to make. Julia's parents don't die. Julia's parents don't keep secrets. She's the better friend because she has to be. I need her more.

We link arms and start the walk back.

"Tomorrow night, let's sleep over at my house," Julia says.

I slept at her house two nights ago. And two nights before that. Ever since Adam left at the beginning of summer, Mom has been letting me sleep over there more and more.

It's a relief, usually, to be away from my heartbroken mom who forgets all her rules and comes down extra hard on mine.

But after being at Julia's more than I'm at my own home for weeks, I'm starting to feel a little weird about it. I'm sick of being a guest so much of the time. And I bet Julia's parents are sick of having a guest all the time.

"I bet there's a graveyard near me somewhere that we can search. I'll Google it."

And suddenly I don't care if her parents want me there or not.

* * *

When Julia leaves the next morning, I sit down at the piano that's pushed against the wall of our dining room.

This is the most peaceful spot in our house for me. It's the only place I can be myself without hiding. Mom loves that I love the piano. Of course she has a whole list of rules about how much I must practice and which pieces I should learn to expand my talent. But I never mind these rules.

I play a few scales, my fingers dancing up and down the keys while I think about what song I want to play first.

My mom appears behind me like she always does when I start to play.

"Oh, good," she says. She starts the timer. She doesn't need to, though. I know I'm going to play long past my required time. I can already tell it is that kind of morning. A piano morning.

I have to get in all the playing I can before I go to Julia's to sleep over tonight. Julia's house doesn't have a piano. It's the only way my house is better than hers.

Mom sits on the tiny couch in the living room adjacent to the room I'm in. She shuts her eyes, which means she's going to sit there and listen to me play today.

She doesn't know it, but I choose what to play based on how I'm feeling.

When I'm happy I play this great mashup of Disney songs. The big, boisterous showstoppers like "Under the Sea" and

"Be Our Guest" and "Do You Want to Build a Snowman?" I learned all the songs with my piano teacher, but I put them all together myself, figuring out how to weave one into the other and then back again so it fills you with all the happy dancing cartoon characters you've ever seen until it's impossible to sit still.

When I'm angry I play Beethoven's Fifth Symphony of course, banging my fingers against the keys for each satisfying *dun* in all the *dun dun dun dun*s.

When I'm sad, it's harder. Sometimes I play a Broadway ballad like "On My Own" or "Light My Candle."

But today I'm not feeling any of those things. I think about exactly how I'm feeling as my fingers take me through the warm-up. I'm a little sad that the JFC buried behind the McKinleys' house wasn't my dad. But there's something else I'm feeling too. Something bigger.

Because Julia and I are going to find my dad.

We are.

I take my hands off the piano and shake them out. I know just what to play.

I take a deep breath as my fingers find the first few tingling notes to the introduction, and then, even though my mom is sitting behind me, the music overtakes me. My fingers dance up and down the keys to Bach's "Solfeggietto" faster and faster until I cannot think about anything else but the next perfect note in each series of sixteen notes.

The piece is too short. I play it again, making it more perfect than the first time.

Again.

Again.

There's only one feeling that fits Bach's "Solfeggietto."

Determination.

four
WHAT'S WRONG WITH MY MOM?

LATER THAT AFTERNOON, I GO TO Julia's house and we start the search for my dad's grave. It lasts the rest of summer.

The graveyard closest to Julia's house, which is also the graveyard second closest to my house, doesn't have any Jorges or Costas or JFCs or even Franciscos.

"It's OK," Julia says. "We'll keep looking."

I can see how she hates walking into graveyards. I can feel her heart racing with fear whenever we lean over a headstone to read it properly.

We spend the long days of August riding our bikes all over our Pittsburgh suburb searching graveyards. We run out and start to ride into neighboring towns. All of this happens because I spend more and more and more time at Julia's house.

My mom is acting stranger and stranger. She's always worked from home, but now she never leaves. She's spending all day every day by herself and can't seem to find room for anything—even me—in our house. She says she'll tell me what she's working on, some big, exciting project, soon enough. But I can't count on that, because she never tells me anything. Instead she keeps dropping me off at Julia's house.

Looking for my dad keeps me from thinking about how weird it is that Julia's mom has started to pretend I'm also her daughter when we're out in public somewhere. And it keeps me from thinking about my mom and Adam and all his promises that went away as soon as he did.

On the few nights when I am home, I stay tucked into my room, out of my mom's way. I don't want to see the way her hair is loose after years of tight buns. I don't want to notice when she misses some part of our daily routine. I don't want to see her coming apart. Instead, I sit at my desk and I write. I fill up one scrap of paper and then another. I cannot keep up with all the questions in my head. Paper questions fill my desk drawers and the corner of my underwear drawer. They pile up under my pillow and mattress. They fill the pockets of my school bag. They take over my room the way they've taken over me.

I start burying questions in some of the random graveyards, even when we don't find my dad.

In each new graveyard I manage to sneak away from Julia for a few minutes and bury a new question.

Where are you?

Where is Adam?

What's happening to Mom?

What happens when you die if your loved ones can't find you?

Why did YOU have to be the one who died?

He's under the earth somewhere. Maybe whoever I'm asking can pass the question to him so he can answer them all when I finally find him.

The days get shorter and summer starts winding to a close. Julia gets her sixth grade letter telling her she's in Mr. Hendricks's class for next year, our last year before middle school. I don't get mine for days because I don't go home and when I do unearth it from a pile of mail on the little coffee table in our living room. I shove it into my pocket, unopened. I'm scared I'll get another teacher. Julia and I have been in the same class the past two years. I'm sure this year I won't be as lucky. I'm too scared to imagine sixth grade without Julia.

Julia starts to complain that we aren't doing anything fun and we run out of graveyards to search, so I try to pretend to be a regular girl. For the last few weeks of summer, we go to the pool and the mall and the ice cream shop. I pretend to be having fun, but I keep thinking about my dad under the ground somewhere. Waiting for me.

In the last week of summer, I spend two full days at home, and then I'm back on Julia's doorstep.

I should be standing with my own mother. Instead, Julia and I flank her mother inside her front door while mine stands on the stoop outside.

"Thank you so much for taking her again," my mom is saying. The sun is shining behind her back, making all the little flyaways of her hair sparkle around her head. She looks angelic and messy all at once. An angelic mess.

I don't know what my mom is doing all by herself all the time. I don't know why that's how she wants it to be. It's like she's craving loneliness. After a lifetime of her constantly on top of me, providing me "structure" at every minute of every day, I don't know how to handle this new version of her.

I feel Julia's mom's arm come down over my shoulders, like she can tell how this is hurting me even though my mom won't let herself see it.

"It's our pleasure," Julia's mom says. "Alma is wonderful to have around."

I wrinkle my nose so that my glasses readjust. Mom shifts from side to side. Her bra straps stick out on either side of the blue tank top she's wearing. Her hair is long and wavy like mine, swinging behind her back. It's disconcerting to see her without her bun.

I need my mom to say something back. Something like, "Yes, of course she is." Or "You know, you're right, what was I thinking, I'm going to take Alma home right now." Or even "I love Alma too, it's just lately . . ."

She skips over the part I need to hear. "It's just lately I've had this project that . . . well, Alma isn't . . . well . . ." Mom's eyes are getting glassy. She's very good at making people feel bad for her when she's asking for help.

I'm already the shortest person standing on this stoop. Mom's mumbling makes me shrink another inch.

"It's OK, Mercy," Julia's mom says. "Listen, I have to take the girls with me to work later. I have some patients coming in the afternoon. Julia usually hangs out with her iPad in the waiting room. I sometimes let her wander into town for Dunkin' Donuts."

"Whatever you say, Beverly," Mom says. She has no opinion. This is so new. It's like her loneliness ate all her opinions.

I run a hand down the frizzy waves of my hair and look up at her. I beg her with my eyes to look at me, smile at me. Just one look and I'll feel so much better today.

"OK, then," Julia's mom says. "You get going. I know you have a lot going on."

Mom doesn't look away from her. She keeps her eyes glassy. "I can't tell you how much I appreciate it."

Julia's mom shifts her weight on her feet. "Just remember, school starts on Monday." She pauses. Then adds, "So tomorrow night is a school night."

Mom nods. "I know," she says. Then she leans through the doorway and plants a kiss on my forehead like it's bedtime. "I love you," she says. "That's why I'm doing what I'm doing."

It's a slightly different refrain. She loves me and that's why she's *doing* what she's *doing*? Why she's dropping me off again like she can't stand to have me around? Why she's working on some mysterious project I can't know anything about?

Because she loves me?

I don't say anything.

I watch through Julia's front door as her halo-frizz disappears into her car. I never knew I could miss her tight bun.

Julia's mom should have explained that "school night" means no more sleepovers. She should have said it directly: my mom can't drop me off and leave day after day after day anymore once school starts. Mom probably didn't realize that's what she meant. Probably in two days I'm going to stand on this doorstep while my mom tries to pass me off and the woman who has been acting like my mom all summer says, "No, not today."

Julia shuts the door and does a happy dance. "Yes!" she says. "Another sleepover! Another sleepover!"

I love Julia.

"Lunch in an hour," Julia's mom says.

"OK!" Julia says. She's already pulling me into her room, a huge smile plastered on her face.

"Be ready to leave for my office when lunch is over," Julia's mom calls behind us.

Julia's mom works as a dermatologist in Parkville. We haven't been to Parkville yet. I know what we're going to do there. And I know Julia isn't going to like it.

Once her bedroom door is shut, Julia plugs her iPod into her speakers and I lunge for her desk chair and open the internet on her laptop. Julia spins in front of me, dancing a little to the Taylor Swift song she just turned on. Julia is all arms and legs, tall and skinny, just the opposite of me. Her hair is sleek and always in a bump-free ponytail. She only wears glasses at night because her mom got her contact lenses last year, and even when she does, her glasses are small and square and black. She usually looks so much older than me.

But I don't mind. I like my bright green glasses with huge lenses. I like that my hair looks a little different every day. I like that my hair isn't a definite color, somewhere between brown and black and red, and that my eyes are a sort of cat-like shape that my mom calls "particularly Portuguese." I like looking different than my best friend.

"What should we do today?" Julia asks.

Then she sees the screen I opened on her computer.

It's a map.

She stops dancing.

"No," she says. "No, Alma, come on. Not today."

"There's one right across the street from the Dunkin' Donuts near your mom's office!" I say, pointing to the Google Earth photo of a graveyard.

"Alma!" she says. "I don't—"

"Look!" I interrupt her, still pointing. "Look how close! It's a sign!"

I wave frantically around the screen. I've zoomed in almost as far as you can go. All you can see is the street angled across the laptop screen. On the lower corner of the screen it says Dunkin' Donuts. On the upper corner it says First Presbyterian Cemetery.

"Right across the street!" I say again.

"That's a main highway," Julia says. Julia doesn't believe in signs.

I shrug.

"My mom will never let us go there," she says. I do feel bad about the way her shoulders are drooping. The spring in her step is gone. Five minutes ago she was joyful at the sight of me. Now I'm scaring her again.

But I have to go. I have to at least look. What if this is the one?

"Your MOM?" I squeal. I laugh a little. I make myself seem big so that she'll have to agree with me. I do what my mom does. "We're not going to tell her."

"Alma," she says. Then she stops. She drops onto her lime-green bedspread. Her room is exactly like her, all bright colors, sleek, sophisticated, cheerful. She has posters of giraffes and magazine ads of giraffes and *National Geographic* pictures of giraffes taped to the wall above her bed and framed pictures displaying me and her family lined up on her desk. A map of Korea hangs on the back of her door and recently she's added some cutouts of Korean characters to the giraffe collection. I don't know what they say.

A normal room for a girl with a normal family.

My room is nothing like this one. It's all white and beige with almost nothing on the walls. And it's full of scraps of paper with questions written in my handwriting. Crowding the corners of every drawer. Wedged in between the pages of my books. Squished between my pillow and my mattress. My room, like me, only pretends to be normal.

"Alma," Julia says again.

I pause and look at her. I raise my eyebrows. "You know I need to look."

"Yeah, but . . ." Julia's voice edges toward whining. "Can't we do something fun today? Summer's almost over."

I point out the window. Dark clouds are rolling over Julia's house. It's so windy that we can see the undersides of the leaves in the trees in her yard. "It doesn't look like summer anyway."

"That doesn't make me want to hang out with dead people!" Julia says.

"We'll go quickly, OK?" I make my eyes do that glassy thing like Mom. Then I say, "You don't have to go with me if you don't want to. I'll figure out a way to go on my own."

"Hmm," Julia says. She waits just a beat too long. "Of course I'll go with you."

I flash her a huge smile, leap out of my seat, and hug her, squeezing my arms around her elbows and pushing my face into her shoulder. "You're the best friend ever!" I say.

We both collapse onto her bed, humming along to Taylor.

"I'm changing the subject," she says, scooting a bit away from me so we're sitting side by side on her bed, but not touching. I wonder if that was normal girl behavior or if she had to scoot away from me because even though I'm her best friend, she's a little scared of me.

"OK," I say.

"Do you have it today?"

It takes me a minute to remember what she's talking about. "Oh!" I say. "Yeah, of course." I pull the sealed envelope from the back pocket of my jean shorts.

Julia puts it in both of her hands and studies the front where my mom's name and my address are printed. She turns it over to where PS 125: New Bridges Elementary School is printed above the flap.

"Ready?" she says. She slips a finger into the corner as if she's going to open it but I yell "NO!"

Julia jumps, startled.

The regular panic is setting in. Now that Julia was in my fourth grade class and my fifth grade class, it's impossible to remember what school was like without her in the same room all day every day. And yet, I know we won't be so lucky three years in a row. There's no way we'll have the same sixth grade teacher. So I've been putting it off, shoving it off.

Fifth grade was the year I lost Adam.

If sixth grade becomes the year I lose Julia . . .

"But tomorrow is the last day of summer," Julia says.

"I know," I say.

Her eyes dig into me. "Please?" Julia begs.

She always says she wants to be in the same class just as much as I do. She says she needs it just as much as I do. She says I'm the only one who gets her and that makes sense because we're the different ones. Julia's different because she was born in Korea and then adopted by her white Pittsburgh-suburbs family. I'm different because my dad is Portuguese and after he died we moved to Florida, then we moved back here. So yes, we're both different. But Julia's life got normal after she was adopted and I'm not adopted so my life is going to stay screwed up. I know I need her more than she needs me. I'm the worse friend, and the needier one.

"Let's open it tonight," I say. "After it gets dark. When it won't be so bad if we cry."

"Alma!" Julia says. "We won't be crying. You'll get Mr. Hendricks too." She says this like she knows even though there's no way to know. She says it like a girl who's used to having everything work out.

I shrug. "Tonight," I say.

Julia holds the letter tight and for a second it looks like she may open it anyway. But, because she's the better friend, she hands it over. "OK," she says. "Tonight."

five
WHY IS LIFE SO UNFAIR?

AN HOUR AND A HALF LATER we're in the graveyard. A shiver runs up my spine and dances around the roots of my hair. I love those shivers, but I can't enjoy it fully because I feel extra bad for dragging Julia here. The dark clouds in the sky make it almost feel like night. Most of the trees in this graveyard don't have any leaves, as if they're as dead as the bodies rotting among their roots. They spread black across the gray sky, looking like arms and spines hunching over the dead grass.

We're the only two people here. Usually, during the day, graveyards have lots of people. People praying. People sitting and talking to a tombstone. People walking their dogs. This one is empty. It's full of old forgotten graves.

A bit of hope mixes in with the warm wind that's whipping around our hair.

"You check the ones closest to the path," I say.

Julia is biting her lip and studying her bright purple rain boots.

"I'll go to the ones down the hill." I point about ten yards away.

"Really?" Julia says, her voice wavering. I call this her Graveyard Voice. She has a Graveyard Voice, which is high and shaky and scared. I should stop making her come to graveyards with me. "Don't you think we should stick together for this one?"

I watch her purple rain boot turn on its side, then right itself. I hesitate. I know I should stay with her. I know that's the good best friend thing to do. But there's that tugging on my heart, like a finger has hooked itself behind my rib cage and it's pulling me heart-first down the hill.

"I'll be right there, where I can see you," I say. "Ten minutes. Then we'll go get Coolattas."

She stares. I have to do something to make her feel OK.

"It's not that bad, Jules," I snicker. "They're already dead. They can't hurt anyone."

Then I walk away, shaking my head. Even I don't believe myself. The dead hurt everybody, just by being dead.

After about ten steps, I check over my shoulder. She's hunched over a gravestone, reading, her black ponytail dancing in the wind behind her. I only let the guilt seize me for a second before I start digging.

"I hope you can get this to my dad," I whisper to the headstone. It says Gloria MacAvee. She died in 1992.

I open the earth near where her hand would be. But that's as far as I get before thunder claps loud enough to make the branches on the ground bounce around us. Lightning spreads a neon spiderweb across the black sky.

"AAALLLLMMMMMAAAA!" Julia screams, not caring about the dead who are all resting and missing their daughters around her. "WE'RE LEAVING! NOW!"

I close my eyes for half a second. I barely got to read any of the graves. I feel for my heart. There's no tugging. The goose bumps are only from the chill in the air.

He's not here.

"Ms. MacAvee," I whisper. "Please get this question to my dad."

Will I ever find you?

The paper is getting wet.

I shove it into the tiny hole and throw some dirt on top of it.

I pause long enough for the sky to open up. Rain falls in one huge sheet, drenching the entire graveyard and everyone in it—dead and alive—all at once. I can't help laughing. I rush at Julia and grab her hand and she grabs me back. We sprint toward the highway, laughing and shrieking and holding on to each other, puddles blooming under our rain boots.

That night we're in Julia's kitchen with her parents, home-made pizzas between us. Bradley, Julia's brother, comes pounding up the stairs. Food is being passed. Days are being discussed. I'm quiet like I always am at Family Dinner with not-my-family.

I lean back on their words. I let the words surround me like walls. I let them hold me up. Because Family Dinner is a thing you hear about. A thing every kid is supposed to have. And this is the closest I come to having it.

I know I don't belong here. All of this isn't really mine. But I take a bite of cheesy pizza and let the warmth spread through and around me. I borrow Julia's family the way I borrow her clothes. It's another thing that makes her a better friend than I am.

I don't have a family for her to borrow back.

"I don't understand how you two got so soaked going to Dunkin' Donuts," Julia's mom says.

My face burns.

It's my fault of course. All my questions are going to get Julia in trouble too.

"It was raining hard, Mom," Julia says, reaching to dish herself some salad. She says it like it's nothing. She didn't used to lie like that.

I think I taught her.

"It looked like it took you guys half an hour to walk the three minutes between Dunkin' Donuts and my office!" Julia's mom says, but with a laugh.

"Mom!" Julia says. "We just—"

Her mom interrupts her. "It's OK, sweetie," she says. "I remember. When you have a best friend, everything becomes an adventure. Even a three-minute walk in the rain."

It's nicer than my mom would say it, but in the end it means the same thing. We were off being silly little girls. Having adventures. Doing unimportant things in the middle of a rainstorm.

Everyone wants me to be that girl. I don't know how.

Well, everyone except my dad.

"So are you ready for sixth grade?" Julia's mom says.

The doorbell rings before we can answer. Julia's dad leaps up and says, "That'll be for me. I'm going out to watch the game tonight."

"Don't run out like that," Julia's mom says. "Invite him in for a minute."

Julia's dad freezes, half in, half out of his seat. His eyes fall on me.

"Oh," Julia's mom says.

Both her parents stop moving and stare at me for a full minute. My heart stops. All of me stops. I freeze with a slice of pizza halfway to my mouth.

Julia's dad leaves the room without saying anything else. I hear the front door open. Then "Hey!" in that voice.

My hands start to tremble. I've been longing for that voice. I've been aching for that voice. And the second I hear it it's like nails in my ears, it hurts so badly.

My heart yanks itself into a million pieces. My legs make me stand up and march me to the top of the stairs.

Below me, I watch Adam and Julia's dad hug.

I should have known this would happen eventually. Adam and Julia's dad are brothers. Adam is Julia's uncle. My mom met Adam through Julia's parents.

But to me they've always seemed so separate.

I'm not ready to see him on the doorstep of the wrong house, but he looks up and sees me.

He looks startled for a second. I see his graying black eyebrows bunch over his blue eyes. I see his jaw drop. Maybe there's some pain. Maybe it's just shock.

He says, "Alma."

I've heard my name in his voice hundreds of times. Millions. Cheering at my soccer games and piano recitals. Waking me up in the morning for school. Handing me my plate at the dinner table. It sounds different now. Like it shouldn't belong to me anymore. Like the sound of my name in his voice traveled through time to reach me here, on Julia's stairs.

Julia's mom is behind me at the top of the stairs now.

"Come on in, Adam," she says. "Henry made pizzas."

Julia's dad, Julia's mom, and Adam all look at me a little too hard and a little too long after she says this. It makes my bones feel electric. I feel powerful and dangerous. They can act like it's something else, but at this moment I know it. Whether Adam has dinner with us is up to me.

Part of me wants it. To sit at the table in Julia's house and pretend it's the table in mine. To sit next to him and have him tell me all about the intricacies of professional soccer as if it's two years ago and I'm sort of interested and sort of just happy to have something close to Family Dinner happening in my own house. But also, this isn't my own house. And the thought of Adam and me having dinner with some other family while my mom is alone doing who-knows-what in the empty house that we all used to share makes me so itchy I want to take my skin off and wash it and hang it up to dry before I eat anything.

I open my mouth to say no. Instead I say, "Where did you go? Why did you leave? Are you ever coming back?"

The questions fall out of me. They make all the adults stand up a little straighter.

Adam climbs the stairs to me. He puts his hands on my shoulders. "You have to ask your mom that, sweetie," he says.

"I want you to tell me," I whisper.

My face is on fire. My knees are shaking. I pretend the whispering protects me. I pretend all the other people in the room can't hear my pain.

"I wish I could," Adam says.

"Then tell me," I say.

Adam stands still like that, with his hands on my shoulders and his mouth hanging open. It's like he wants to say something but my mom locked away all of his words.

I don't know how long the silent staring lasts. It feels like years. Finally Julia's dad says, "Well, I did make pizza, but also it's twenty-five-cent wings night at Corby's." They both laugh, as if that's funny somehow.

"Go ahead," Julia's mom says. "Have fun. Go Pirates."

"Alma," Adam says. He stands up straighter on the stairs. He holds out his arms. "Come here, kiddo."

I lean forward, just slightly. I leave some space between our shoulders. I don't come close enough for him to hug me.

I want him to hug me. I don't want to want him to hug me.

"It's good to see you," he says. But it sounds sad. Like seeing me actually messed up his day.

He pats me on the head.

Then he's gone. I stare at the closed door a little too long.

My heart is still broken. Shattered. Bits of it are spreading and poking all over my body: my fingers and knees and rib cage.

I shake myself, as if that can put the pieces back together, and then go and join not-my-family for the rest of dinner.

"Alma," Julia's mom says when I sit next to her. She puts her hand on mine. "Are you all right?"

I shake her off. "I'm fine!" I say. It's loud and rude. I don't mean to be loud and rude. Julia deserves a fun and regular and polite best friend. Somehow she got stuck with me.

"So, sixth grade," Julia's mom says, ignoring my rudeness. "Last year before middle school!"

Julia and I nod.

"I want to see honor roll report cards all four quarters this year!" She acts like she's talking to me too, but I've never shown Julia's mom my report card.

Sometimes when I sit at this table, I want to explode. I'm so angry. It's so unfair.

"Who's your sixth grade teacher, Alma?"

I shrug.

"She still won't open her letter!" Julia says. "But I know it'll be OK. I know she got Mr. Hendricks."

Julia's mom tilts her head at me. Her blue eyes seem to stare through mine, to the back of my brain, like she can read the thoughts being traded on my synapses. "You know Julia will still be your best friend even if you have a new teacher, right?"

"Of course," I say. But it doesn't matter because she can see my invisible shrug.

six

WHY DO GOOD THINGS HAPPEN TO BAD PEOPLE?

A FEW HOURS LATER WE'RE IN Julia's room sitting cross-legged in our pajamas on the lime-green bedspread with the closed envelope between us. The giraffes on her wall watch us.

"Do you want to know what my parents said about Uncle Adam and your mom?" Julia asks.

I raise my eyebrows. "Your parents talked about it?" I say.

"Well, I asked," Julia says.

Acid sloshes in my stomach. Julia knows more about my family than I do.

"They said that your mom and Adam used to love each other romantically, like they used to be in love. But then they realized they fell out of love. And that sometimes that happens. And that it's sad. But they still love each other as friends."

"Oh," I say. Because that's no information at all. That's the kind of thing grown-ups tell you to make it sound like they're answering your questions, but when you really think about it you realize it's all words and no answers.

"And they also said it's not your fault," Julia says. "But that you may be a little more sad more often than usual. Because you miss Adam."

I'm itchy again, and I don't know what to say, so I change the subject.

"What does that say?" I ask, pointing to Julia's closed bedroom door. She's hung a new poster there in the past few days. It's a scene of a Korean city with something in Korean written above it.

"I don't know," Julia says, faster and louder than she usually talks. "I don't read Korean. How would I know Korean?"

"Oh," I say. She won't look at me. I said the wrong thing somehow. "Let's open the school letter," I say finally.

"OK!" Julia says in her regular voice. Then she pauses. "No matter what this says, you'll meet me at the swing set as soon as recess starts Monday, right?" Julia asks.

"Right," I say.

"We'll still be best friends even with different teachers, right?"

"Right," I say.

"Promise?" Julia asks.

"Promise," I say.

It feels good for her to make me promise when I want to make her promise the same thing.

It's not like she's leaving you, I tell myself. *It's not like Adam. It's not even like Mom.*

I have a hard time believing it. It feels like once I read this letter I'll lose Julia and her mom and dad too. She'll find a new best friend. A normal girl. I'll be left with no one except my dead father.

"Here we go." She sighs. "Open it."

She closes her eyes and crosses her fingers over her heart. "Mr. Hendricks. Mr. Hendricks. Mr. Hendricks," she mumbles.

I slip a finger under the edge of the envelope and wiggle it until the glue loosens. I pull the paper out and unfold it.

Julia keeps whispering, "Mr. Hendricks. Mr. Hendricks."

I open the paper and scan it quickly. "Oh!" Then my jaw drops.

"What?" Julia says, dropping her fingers and opening her eyes. "What!" she says again.

I turn the paper around so she can read it.

"Mr. Hendricks!" she squeals. "Mr. Hendricks!"

She springs off the floor and throws her arms around me, tackling me into the white carpet on her bedroom floor.

"Three years in a row!" she cries.

I'm still stunned speechless. I don't deserve good news like this, I don't think. But here it is. In my hands.

Through her closed bedroom door, we hear the front door open and shut. Her dad is home. The baseball game must be over.

For a second I wonder if Adam is with Julia's dad. I imagine them both hugging us over our good news. Two different dads for two different girls.

Except Adam isn't my dad.

Julia runs to her bedroom door, flings it open, and screams down the hall, "We're in the same class!"

"All right!" her dad's voice echoes back. He's alone.

That night as I lie in my sleeping bag on Julia's floor for the millionth time this summer, I can't stop thinking about Adam. About how he acted like my dad. About how he cooked me breakfast and signed me up for soccer clinics and came to them and cheered louder than the other dads. About how after a while I stopped thinking about how he wasn't my real dad.

About his Bold Idea and how it disappeared.

"Alma," Adam had said. It was April of fifth grade. We were at the diner at the end of our block having burgers and milkshakes. Adam was letting me take sips of his chocolate malt even though I had a cookies-n-cream one all to myself.

"Alma . . . Alma . . ." He'd said my name over and over again. Almost like he was nervous.

I looked at my milkshake and smoothed my frizzy hair over the arm of my glasses, trying to make him more comfortable by not looking in his eyes.

My mom was shifting around in the seat next to me. I could feel her heart beating more quickly. Either she didn't know what he was trying to say, or she didn't like it.

"Alma," he said a final time before pushing on. "I want to ask you something. It's a big, important question. In fact, it's a rather bold idea. And I want you to know that whatever answer you give is fine."

"Adam," Mom had said. "You don't have to—"

He'd looked at her. His blue eyes had never looked so serious. "Mercy, I do," he'd said. "I do have to."

He'd looked back at me. "Alma," he'd said. "Here it is. I love you more than I ever knew I could love a kid. I love you more than I love myself."

My mouth dropped open. I guess I already knew Adam loved me. He showed me all the time by taking my picture and coaching my soccer team and signing me up for the community choir and picking me up from Julia's house. But him saying it like that, it felt different. It felt solid.

I didn't know how to answer. I couldn't say anything so solid. "I . . . me . . . me too," I'd stumbled.

"You just listen, OK, sweetie?" he'd said. "You're going to need a few days to think about what I'm going to ask you anyway."

"OK," I'd said.

"So Alma, here's my bold idea: I'd like to be your father. Your second father. I'd never erase the man who made you, but . . . Well, there's a thing called stepparent adoption. And I think you deserve a father who is here now. Who can do things for you. And . . . I love you like you're my own. You *are* mine. I could never love a kid more. So . . . I'd like to adopt you."

My eyes had gone wide. My heart had sparked little

fireworks that rushed all over my bloodstream. I was pretty sure I was happy but it was a different sort of feeling than I'd ever had before so I couldn't exactly tell.

My mom's heart was beating too fast next to me. I could feel her head going back and forth in a "no" motion. Like she knew what I'd say.

But I didn't think too much about my mom. Instead, I pictured the JFC headstone. I pictured Jorge Francisco Costa. In my imagination, I asked his permission.

"Alma," he'd say. "I'll always be your father. But you deserve a dad. An alive dad. A dad who can make you blueberry pancakes and take you to piano lessons."

I opened my eyes and looked right into Adam's. He was right. Except for my mother, I'd never been so sure that anyone loved me. His eyes practically had firework-hearts dancing out of them, sailing to meet the fireworks spinning all over my bloodstream.

"I think—" I started.

But Mom interrupted me. "You heard Adam," she said. "And he's right. You should take a day or two. Take the weekend. Give your answer on Monday."

But by Monday the question was gone. And by June, so was Adam.

The sun is starting to sink by the time Julia's mom drops me off in front of my house the next day. It's a good reminder that fall is coming. And then winter. My mom will put me back on a schedule. She'll go back to checking my homework. She'll go back to timing how long I practice the piano every day. She's been strict about school since I was in kindergarten. I never knew I could miss the strictness.

"Hello!" I call when I walk in the door. I quickly shove my Target bags in the hall closet. Julia's mom took us shopping earlier in the day, so I bought all my school supplies: binders and pens and highlighters and note cards. I'm excited to get to my room and write on all the little binder tabs and put all my pens and pencils into my pencil case and put batteries in my new calculator. Last year Mom stood over me and made me do these things when there were still weeks left of summer. This year she hasn't said a word about school.

"Hello!" I say again. I know my mom is home. She works from home. She relaxes at home. She does big mysterious projects at home. She's never not home unless she's dropping me off somewhere.

I walk through the entrance hall to the living room. Mom is sitting on the little off-white couch, surrounded by papers. There's a notebook spread on the glass coffee table in front of her and a calendar to her left. There are printed papers in piles all over the couch and table and even the floor. Mom presses her cell phone to her ear and holds up a finger to tell me to hold on a second. Her hair hangs long over the phone.

But I'm not looking at her. I'm looking at the empty space in front of her where the rust-colored armchair used to be. It was just there yesterday. Now it's gone. There are scratch marks on the hardwood where the four legs used to sit. The floor it used to cover is a little pale and even more dusty than the rest of the room. It was my favorite chair.

"I'll have to call you back," Mom says. "My daughter just got home."

She hangs up.

"That was Nanny and PopPop," she says to me.

I turn to look at her. I don't even bother to point out that she just lied. She wouldn't call me "my daughter" to Nanny and PopPop. Plus, they would have asked to talk to me.

"Where's the chair?" I ask.

This is probably a Bad Question. I ask it anyway.

Mom starts shuffling papers.

"Which chair?" she says.

Things have been disappearing all summer. First it was the TVs and Mom said that was because we needed fewer screens around here and I still had my tablet and my laptop so I didn't worry too much about that. Then it was the oriental carpet in the living room, which Mom said was Adam's and that he came to get it. And I didn't worry too much about that either even though no one ever officially told me that the divorce was final and Adam had moved out and wasn't coming back.

Then it was the rug in my room. Mom said she met someone at work who really needed a rug.

Then it was the dining room table and chairs. I stopped asking.

Then it was my floor lamp. The painting of Lisbon that

usually hangs in the front hallway. The living room floor lamp. The slow cooker in the kitchen. The bigger couch in the living room.

Then almost everything that had been hanging on the walls.

The rocking chair that was in Mom and Adam's room.

Now my favorite chair.

Our living room looks ridiculous now: one small couch and one small coffee table, shoved into the corner of a huge space. It opens right into the dining room, which has nothing in it but the piano. It looks like we just moved in and haven't had time to get settled.

"I loved that chair," I say.

Mom shakes her head and stands, papers falling all around her. She walks over and hugs me.

I let her, even though I don't want to. I let her, even though I wanted to hug Adam yesterday and I didn't let him.

"It had to go," she says. "It was older than you are."

"I'm only twelve," I say. Twelve isn't old if you're a chair.

But her hug is working. I reach up and hug her back. I sink into the soft folds of her. I say "I'm only twelve" again. But this time I mean it differently. Twelve is still young enough to miss your mom when you've spent most of the summer at your best friend's house for no real reason.

Mom pulls back, looks at me, and smiles. It feels good. It feels good to be someone's real daughter instead of promising a woman who will never see my report card that I'm going to try for the honor roll.

Or talking to a ghost who loves me.

"Don't question me," she says. "I can't explain every detail. I don't have time." She glances back toward whatever she's been working on.

I pull the envelope from my pocket where I've been storing it. She will like this envelope. It has answers instead of questions. "Guess what?" I say. "I got Mr. Hendricks!"

"Hmm?" Mom says, but she's already turning back to her piles of paper on the coffee table.

"The same teacher as Julia!"

Mom bends down to look at something. "Well, that would be nice, huh?" she mumbles.

But she's gone. Already texting someone with one hand while pointing to her calendar with the other.

She didn't hear me. My head hurts. "Is there dinner?" I ask.

It's 6:05. For my entire life, dinner has been at 6:00 p.m. sharp.

"Mmmm," Mom says. "Frozen pizza in the freezer. Hungry?" But she doesn't look up.

"It's OK," I mumble. "I can do it."

"Thanks," she says.

It is the last night of summer, the night before school. Last year this night, I was the same. I was full of Bad Questions. I was missing my dead dad even though Mom wanted me to forget all about him.

Still, Mom paid attention to me. She wrote my name on all

my binders and checked my backpack three times to be sure
I had packed it correctly. Adam brought home my favorite
burgers from the diner and we all sat together while he told
us about all the pranks he had pulled on his own fifth-grade
teacher.

It's the last night of summer. This year I warm up frozen
pizza for myself, go into my own room, lay out my outfit, and
put myself to bed.

I wait in my bed with my lights on. I lie on my side and
watch the red numbers on the digital clock on my nightstand.

9:55

9:59

10:00

10:02

10:15

For the first time ever, my mom does not come and tell me
to turn my lights out.

I fall asleep with them on.

seven

WHO IS ALMA McARTHUR?

I WAKE UP IN THE MIDDLE of the night and my light is still on. I turn over and check my clock.

2:09

My mom really never came. Maybe she's mad at me. Maybe she found the pile of scrap paper with my questions written on them in the corner of my underwear drawer. Maybe that's why she's been making me spend so much time with Julia.

I lie still on my bed and listen for something. Anything. Any sound to show that I'm not completely alone in my loneliness.

It takes a few minutes to figure out what I'm listening for.

Adam.

He used to get up to watch European soccer games in the middle of the night. It drove my mom crazy. She liked everyone to have a bedtime, even Adam. But he used to say it wasn't the same unless he watched the games in real time.

I'd hear him cheering or cursing and I'd tiptoe out of my

bed and find him and his laptop in the burgundy chair in the living room. He'd smile when he saw me. He'd pour me a glass of milk and scoot over in the chair to make room for me. The chair was so big there was plenty of room for both of us if we sat the right way. I'd watch with him for a few minutes.

I never knew what was going on in the game. Without my glasses it just looked like a bunch of colors moving over a green screen. I was too tired to try to make it make sense.

But Adam would put his arm around me and I'd lean back into his chest. I'd match my breath to his and watch the colors dance. Then I'd be sleepy enough to go back to bed.

Other times I'd wake up in the middle of the night and Adam was not in the burgundy chair with a laptop in his lap. Then I'd remember that I'm actually a bad girl and I'd go looking for all the answers a bad girl isn't supposed to have.

I'd eavesdrop.

The last time I did that, I heard a lot. Adam and my mom were fighting again. There had been a lot of fights, but I could tell this one was different. It was a quiet fight and no one was talking about dishes or laundry. This was the fight that all the other fights had been covering up.

"You're not going to tell Alma," Mom had said. There was a band of light under their bedroom door so I pushed my ear against it and listened. "She's too young."

"Do you think she's not going to notice?" Adam yelled. "You think one day I'm not going to be here and she won't start asking questions?"

"She asks questions," Mom said, quiet.

"She asks questions all the time!" Adam yelled. "She asks about her dad almost every day. When are you going to start giving her the answers?"

The fighting had started after Adam had taken me and Mom out to lunch and he'd asked me about the Bold Idea.

"She's too young to think about this stuff, Adam," Mom said.

I hated when she said that. It might be true, I'm too young. I should be making my brain different than it is. But I still think about everything.

"This stuff is the truth," Adam said. "About me. About her father. About herself."

"I don't want her to turn out like . . ." Mom didn't finish.

"Mercy." There was a long pause, and then Adam said, not quite as loud, "I think we're at a crossroads."

"What do you mean?" Mom said.

"I can't . . . I don't think I can live with myself if I have to keep doing what you're asking me to do."

Then I heard Mom crying.

"I understand how this snowballed," Adam said. "But I really think you . . . we . . . you owe her the truth."

It was funny. He was giving me the truth by having this fight. I could see what was coming so clearly, even though I knew Mom wouldn't sit me down and explain it. My friend Sharice said that when her parents got divorced, her mom sat her down and told her. She let Sharice yell and then let her ask questions. I knew that wasn't how my mom would handle it.

Adam would just be gone.

"I'll tell her," Mom said. "I'm just . . . She's not ready."

"I can't do this anymore, Mercy," Adam said.

They were both crying and I was about to cry too.

My dad was dead.

My not-dad was leaving.

There are no sounds in my house tonight, of course. Mom doesn't make noise all by herself. Still, I get out of bed and tiptoe down the hallway toward her room. Her light is still on.

She's awake. Or else she fell asleep with it on, like me.

I press my ear against the door. I hear nothing.

I wonder if her light will stay on all night.

I know mine will.

The next morning all the rain has burned off and I'm sweating through my purple leggings within seconds of showing up at the bus stop. It's too hot for the first-day-of-school outfit I picked out with Julia. I didn't know it would be like ninety degrees at eight in the morning. No one told me, of course, because I haven't seen anyone today.

This morning my mom didn't get up. I made myself some oatmeal, brushed my teeth, got dressed, and then waited outside her door. I stood there and rolled my fingernails against white painted wood, sort of knocking but not loud enough to wake her up if she was sleeping. I knocked hard with my brain. I knocked and knocked in my mind. But it turns out mind-knocking doesn't wake anyone.

I gave up.

If my dad were alive, he'd drive me to school every single day. I'd never have to take the bus. He'd wake up early to make me blueberry pancakes like Julia's dad does. He'd take my picture and then send it to all his friends saying something about how he can't believe his baby is starting the sixth grade. He'd be proud of me.

I feel like the loneliness of this—of the first day of sixth grade with no parent, no picture, no breakfast, no fanfare—is so thick it's hanging around me and making me smell. So maybe it's OK that I'm sweating. I'd rather smell like sweat than like loneliness.

I'm the only one at the bus stop, which is usual because I'm here a few minutes early and that's also how it was last year, just me waiting for the bus most days. But last year Mom and Adam drove me on the first day of school and took my picture. And Adam even waited with me at the bus stop on the second day of school to make sure it came for me.

Now I'm standing in the early morning with the sun beating down on my frizzy hair and the heat radiating off the sidewalk and into my black flats. And I'm alone.

After a few minutes a woman and a younger boy rush down the street, his backpack flying behind him, her hair coming out of her ponytail. "Is this the bus stop?" she asks, all rushed and hurried.

"Yes," I say.

"For PS 125?" she asks.

"Yup," I say.

"Good," the woman says, breathing too hard. "We're new in town and I was worried we would miss it. Here, Jackson," she says. She pulls him over to her and starts smoothing his hair with her palm. "This is Jackson," she says to me.

Jackson is wiggling like crazy, trying to get away from his mom's big hand. He's almost as tall as me even though he's younger.

"I'm a new third grader!" he announces.

"I'm Alma," I say. "Sixth grade."

"What a big girl," Jackson's mom says, grabbing him by the arm and pulling him back to her. "Standing out here by yourself."

"I guess," I say.

"Your mom and dad didn't want to come and see you off on your first day?"

My neck burns and I feel like punching her.

"My dad's dead," I say.

I don't usually say that. I have to be so angry to say that out loud.

I don't think I knew I was quite that angry this morning until I said those words.

"I . . . I'm sorry," the woman says. Jackson breaks loose and runs a few feet away. She looks at me with these gray eyes that are begging me to say "It's OK" and I know I'm supposed to say "It's OK" because she's a grown-up and that's the polite thing. But I don't. I don't say anything. I don't have to be a good girl. I don't even have to pretend to be a good girl. No one is here to make me.

Jackson saves us by shouting "The bus is coming! The bus is coming!" We both look where he's pointing and see the big yellow bus rolling over the hill.

My heart slows with relief.

The bus pulls up and the door creaks open. I step inside as Jackson's mom tries to wrestle him into a hug behind me.

"What's your name?" the bus driver asks me. She's a big, tall woman with blond curls popping out the sides of a white hoodie, which she's wearing even though it's a million degrees on this bus.

"Alma McArthur," I say.

She checks a clipboard hanging by the side of her seat. She mumbles, "Who is Alma McArthur?"

That has to be the worst question of all.

Behind her a girl calls out "Alma!" I glance up and see some faces I remember—Annette and Sharice—girls Julia and I play with at recess or whisper with at lunch, girls who we didn't see all summer. I'm itchy to get past this driver and hug them.

"I'm sorry," the driver says. "I don't have an Alma on my bus. Just one kid at this stop, Jackson Clark."

"That's me," Jackson says. He climbs on the bus and shoves past me.

"I'm sorry. I'm so sorry," his mom is saying behind him.

"But . . . I'm on this bus," I say. "I got a letter and everything."

"I'm sorry, kiddo. I can't drive you to school if your name isn't here on my list."

"But . . . this is my bus stop."

The driver just looks at me.

Behind me kids start to snicker.

"How . . . How am I supposed to get to school?"

"I don't know, kid." The driver moves around in her seat, looking past me. "Is your mom or dad here?"

The sweat on my face is threatening to turn to tears. I'm not angry enough to pull the my-dad-is-dead card anymore. I'm not angry at all. I'm sad. I'm a sweaty, teary mess. The driver sees my almost-tears.

"Go home and talk to your mom, OK?" she says softly. "Is she home?"

I nod. I can't speak or I'll cry.

"Well, tell her to call the school and get it fixed. I'm sure she can work this out."

My mom forgot more than to say good night. She forgot to sign me up for the bus. School has always been the most important thing to her. More than the piano. More than family, even. How did she forget something like this?

I squeak, "OK." But I don't move. I'm frozen.

"I'm sorry, Ms. Alma. I have to ask you to get off the bus now."

The kids behind me laugh. I walk down the steps of the bus

and suddenly I'm on the sidewalk again. Alone.

I trudge home. I'll have to wake up my mom and ask her to drive me to school. Then I'll have to remind her to register me for the bus.

I have no other options.

After a summer without her, Mom is still my only person. My only alive person.

I don't know how to do this, though. I don't know how to be the one who remembers to sign me up for the bus and who makes my own dinner and breakfast and cleans it up. My mom has always been the organized one. I've always been the mess.

I try not to tell myself how this would never have happened if Adam were still living with us.

How this never would have happened if Dad were living with us.

I run across the dead grass in the yard and open our blue front door. I go through the entryway and I'm accosted again by the empty living room, nothing there except a small couch and table covered in papers.

"I don't know," my mom is wailing. She's on the other side of the wall in the kitchen. I freeze and listen as if it's the middle of the night.

"You have to find her!" she yells. "I woke up and she was gone. She's never done anything like this before."

I've never heard Mom sound like this. Out of control.

"Why are you so calm? A twelve-year-old girl is missing!"

She's talking about me?

I shout, "Mom? I'm in here."

"Alma!" she yells. I hear her drop something and then suddenly she's all around me in the biggest, softest, warmest hug of all time. "Alma, Alma, Alma. Don't you ever do that to me again," she says.

"Do what?" I ask, my voice muffled by her shoulder. She's hugging me so tightly my glasses are askew on my nose.

"You scared me half to death! You cannot do that to me. You can't. You hear me?" She pulls back to look at me, then buries me in the hug again. "I can't lose you too. I can't lose you."

But first she says she can't lose me *too*. This is the closest we've come to talking about Adam.

Questions rush through my brain like water out of a dam. All the Bad Questions swirling in me just when my mom is loving me the most. I freeze, hoping she'll say more.

Instead she says, "Where were you?"

Adults are allowed to have questions in this house. Any questions they want. And kids need to answer them. Only adult secrets are good secrets. Kid secrets are all bad.

I have a lot of secrets. This isn't one of them.

"The bus stop," I say.

Her eyes go wide and her voice goes high enough to hit the ceiling. "The bus stop. What? Why? Why would you be at the bus stop? Where? Which one? Where were you trying to go?"

I don't follow her into the panic. She thinks I'm about to get in the most trouble ever. But I'm not. I answer flatly. "School," I say.

"School?" she says. Then she takes a step back and shakes her shoulders a little bit, like she's shrugging off an invisible coat. She's still in faded pink pajamas, not even wearing a robe. I must have really scared her. And I feel bad about it. I feel bad about trying to go to school.

"School," she says, more calm this time. "Why?"

I lower my eyebrows. How do I answer that? Because I'm twelve? Because I'm in the same class with Julia? Because a letter came?

"It's . . . It's the first day," I say. "But you forgot to register me for the bus. You have to drive me."

I'm going to be so late. She won't take me in her pajamas. It'll be almost lunchtime by the time I get there and Mr. Hendricks's whole class will be laughing about how I got rejected by the bus driver.

I'm thinking about all of that so hard I miss what she says.

"What?" I say.

"I never told you to go to school."

"Mom!" I say. "I have to go to school."

"I know," she says. She turns toward the kitchen like the conversation is over.

"Mom!" I say again. "Get dressed! I have to go to school now."

"Alma," she says, still not looking at me and making her

voice all high like what she's going to say is no big deal. But I know when she does this it's always a very big deal whatever she says. "I don't know why you thought you'd be going back to that school."

My heart stops.

"What?" I whisper.

Mom gathers her hair into her two palms. She begins to wind it behind her head. She's putting her bun back.

"I didn't take you to meet your teacher like we did last year. I didn't take you shopping for school supplies. I didn't drive you today like I did last year. Why would you think you were going back to the same school?"

I thought you forgot all those things. I want to say that out loud. But I think it might be worse than a question.

Her bun gets tighter and tighter.

"I'm not going to school?" I ask. My voice is quiet and squeaky. I'm scared.

"Of course you are," Mom says. "School is your job. You're going to go to an excellent school."

"A new school?" I ask.

"I've got it all set up. Of course I didn't forget to sign you up for the bus. I would never forget something like that. I have everything all worked out."

But that makes no sense. She's forgotten lots of things all summer. She forgot to tell me *not* to go to school.

How can I be going to a new school?

How can I have no say over what happens to me?

My hands are shaking.

I open my mouth but Mom cuts me off before any sounds come out. "Don't question me today, Alma," she says. "I really cannot handle it."

I close my mouth.

I try hard to say something.

But my mom looks like a stranger in pink pajamas. Maybe it's that I haven't seen the tight bun in weeks. Maybe it's that she's making coffee and not on her phone or shuffling through endless piles of paper.

"Do not stand there and stare at me, Alma. Please go practice piano. I'll set the timer."

Or maybe it's just that I've seen so little of her for months and months. Maybe we forgot how to be a family.

eight

WHERE IS ALL THE FURNITURE?

THE FIRST TIME I VISITED A graveyard I was five years old. I was with my mother. And I made a big mistake.

A coworker of my mom's had died, but I didn't know that because that wasn't how she told me.

All I knew was that Lucy, my babysitter from down the street, had texted my mom and then my mom was all upset. Suddenly, she was putting me in my heavy winter dress, which was dark purple. She pulled black tights onto my legs. It was July. She said I didn't have anything else appropriate to wear and I would just have to be hot. She said it like it was my fault.

She strapped me into my booster seat and drove off without explaining anything. She was mumbling to herself about Lucy canceling and never having any help and everything being too hard. We pulled into a parking lot and Mom turned around and stared at me.

I knew something was weird. Something had been weird

for days. I stayed as still as possible while she talked.

"This isn't really a place for children," she said.

I made my eyes not look out the window at the building we were sitting next to. I was only five, but even then I knew that church was a fine place for children.

"But I have to be here, and Lucy canceled, so I have to bring you with me." She paused. "Do you understand?"

I nodded, a tiny movement of my head.

"You need to stay as still and as quiet as possible and . . . and try not to listen. There may be some sad people here, but don't worry about them, OK? Don't look at them."

I didn't move.

"My purse is full of jelly beans," she said. "You eat them one at a time. You hide them from everyone. I want you to sit through this and think about jelly beans. Nothing else. Don't worry about anyone but you. Don't think about anyone or anything but jelly beans."

"Why will people be sad?" I asked.

Mom had been sad a lot. She'd stayed home from work yesterday and I'd heard her crying when I was supposed to be playing with Lucy. But when I asked she told me she wasn't sad.

Sometimes I felt like sad and bad were the same things. When I was sad Mom was so upset about it, it was basically the same as when I was being bad.

"Think about jelly beans," Mom said.

Mom always told me what I should and shouldn't think

about. Sometimes other thoughts snuck into my brain though.

I nodded.

"When this is all over, we'll go on an adventure, you and me. If you're a good girl and you stay quiet and don't ask any questions, we'll have an adventure."

"OK," I said. "Will we go to Portugal?"

Mom laughed. She always laughed when I asked about going to Portugal, where my daddy had grown up.

"Not yet," Mom said. "A little adventure today. Just us two. We'll go to the trampoline park."

I nodded a lot. "OK!" I said. I loved the trampoline park.

We went into the church. I did everything my mom asked, almost. I sat right next to her. I was still and quiet. I took jelly beans out of her purse one at a time and popped them into my mouth, guessing their colors as they melted on my tongue.

But I couldn't help hearing all the words. I couldn't help thinking about Lisa, whoever she was, and how she was dead now.

This was the second dead person I knew about.

Jelly beans melted on my tongue one after another and I imagined Lisa and my dad meeting in some empty, white room somewhere. They would be talking about how good I was being at Lisa's funeral, eating my jelly beans, staying as quiet as a breathing person could.

There were other children there. They were listening too. One was as small as me. And he sat in front of me and cried and cried and cried. His dad was sitting next to him. His dad didn't even tell him not to cry.

If my dad were here, he'd probably let me cry too.

After it was over, we got back in the car. I didn't say any-thing and I tried not to move in my car seat even though I was all out of jelly beans.

I thought we would go to the trampoline park, but instead Mom followed behind a big black car as it wound through country roads and up a hill covered with the greenest grass I'd ever seen, and through a black gate.

And then I saw them. Rows and rows of headstones. I knew what this was. This was the graveyard. This was where they put dead people. This was where they put my dad.

My heart started tugging everywhere and my dad was sud-denly next to me in the car. I was sure I could see him. He was grown-up and a man but otherwise looked just like me.

"Hi, Alma," he said.

I gasped and he disappeared.

"It's OK, Alma," Mom said. "We just have to get through this part and then you'll be jumping on the trampolines."

I didn't say anything.

"You don't have to be scared," she said.

Except I wasn't scared. I was excited.

It was a lot harder to stay quiet and still at this part of the funeral. I stood next to my mother while my blood danced with sugar and surprise. I couldn't wait to run through this graveyard with her. I would ask her to read every headstone until we could find the one that said *Alma's dad*.

They lowered a box into the dirt and lots of people threw a flower on it. Mom didn't. She watched and held my hand. I tried not to see the grown-ups and the one little boy crying. I tried not to feel as happy as I felt because I knew the people around me were all sad.

And then Mom walked toward the car.

I kept my feet right where they were, my black Mary Janes indenting the wet, green grass.

"Come on, Alma," Mom said.

I wasn't supposed to talk so I just shook my head.

Mom walked back toward me and whispered in my ear. "Alma!" she said. "Let's go."

I shook my head again.

I usually almost always listened to my mom. But I couldn't.

I could feel him everywhere. He was tugging on my heart. He was pulling at my feet, trying to get me to walk. He was playing with my hair.

There was no way I was leaving the graveyard without finding him.

"Alma, I'm warning you," Mom said and turned toward the car.

I looked away, up the hill. I saw hundreds of them. Maybe thousands. White tombstones in all different shapes in all directions. Some looked like curves, some were just squares, some were crosses or angels or other shapes. It might take all day to find the right one. But that was OK.

I didn't need to go to the trampoline park.

"Now," my mom said. "Or else we're not going jumping."

I took a step away from her. By now some people from the funeral were watching, but I didn't care.

I ran to the tombstone closest to Lisa's. Mom ran after me. "What does this one say?" I asked her, pointing.

"I'm not playing, Alma," Mom said.

"What does it say?" I ask again.

"This is not the time for a reading lesson," Mom said. She bent to pick me up.

"No!" I screamed. I tried to catapult myself out of her arms. "No!"

"Alma!" she said. "That's enough!"

I bent backward and managed to fall out of her grasp. I crashed into the grass headfirst and heard voices around me say "Ooh!" That's when I realized lots of people were watching.

I didn't care.

I jumped up and ran in the other direction.

Everyone was watching now. Everyone was listening as I was screaming.

"I'm going to find him! I'm going to find him!"

I stopped at a headstone a few rows away. Mom came stumbling after me, her black heels sticking in the grass.

"Alma Meredith McArthur, you get in the car right now."

I pointed to the headstone. "Tell me what this says!" Then I looked up toward the crowd. "Someone tell me what this says!"

"Alma!" she shouted. "Get! In! The! Car!"

"NO!" I screamed. "TELL ME WHAT THIS SAYS!"

She picked me up again and started to run toward the car. I wiggled and wiggled and wiggled until I almost managed to fall again. I screamed "No! No! NO!" the whole time. "I HAVE TO FIND HIM!"

Finally, she put me down. She held my shoulders between her hands and looked at me with the same look from the car earlier. This time I wouldn't look back. This time I wouldn't be still.

"Tell me," she said. "Tell me quietly."

I stopped squirming.

"What are you looking for?"

I took a deep breath like Ms. Miller at school had shown me. She said whenever you had something big to say, it was a good idea to take a deep breath first.

"My dad," I said.

Mom shook her head slowly.

"Alma, sweetie, your dad isn't here," she said.

"Nanny said!" I yelled back. But my throat hurt. And I was tired. I couldn't squirm as much. "Nanny said he was here!"

"She did?" Mom lowered her eyebrows. "You don't even know where we are. You're only five."

"We're in the graveyard! That's where you put him! Nanny said!" I was crying by now. Mom's eyes looked wet too.

She wrapped me into a big hug and rocked me back and forth. "Sweetie," she said. "He's in a different graveyard. There are lots and lots of graveyards."

"No," I said. But I wasn't screaming now. "No! There's only one."

"There are lots," Mom said. She rocked me and I could feel myself relaxing into her hug even though I didn't want to.

"There's only one! There's only one!"

People started walking away. I was losing my audience. I was trying to be as loud as I had been, but I couldn't.

"He has to be here."

"There are lots, Alma. Lots of graveyards. All over the world," Mom said into my ear.

"There has to be only one," I said. "I have to find him. He's here."

Because if there were lots of graveyards everywhere, if there were lots of graveyards with rows and rows of stones like this one . . . if there were so many . . . I'd never be able to find him.

Mom reached to pick me up. I let her this time. She started walking toward the car and I saw all the heads of all the funeral-goers turn as we walked by the crowd.

Tears fell out of my eyes, soaking Mom's shoulder.

There was no more taste of jelly beans on my tongue. There was no more Good Alma left from in the church.

She strapped me into my booster seat and I fell asleep. When I woke up, Mom was not huggy and soft anymore.

She turned around in the car and said, "That was incredibly inappropriate behavior for a five-year-old. When we get home, you will spend the afternoon in your room thinking about what you did."

I nodded. I didn't feel like jumping anymore anyway.

It's easiest to be a good girl when I'm practicing the piano. Playing the piano is the one thing I love to do that my mom also loves me doing.

I sit at the piano and play for hours. Mom's timer goes off saying I've practiced enough and I just keep on playing. Mom moves around behind me, getting back into her strange paper-obsessed thing she's been doing all summer. Every once in a while she comes and stares over my shoulder, listening to the music, a sad expression on her face.

My mom is allowed to be sad.

I'm not.

I play the saddest song I can think of. I play it twice. I start playing it a third time when my mom comes up behind me. I'm certain she's going to tell me the song is too sad and I shouldn't be playing sad music.

Music has always been the one thing in my control.

"Alma," she says. "I need to make a phone call. Please go somewhere else."

I don't bother to ask why she can't make the phone call in her own room.

I want to go to a graveyard. Even after all those sad songs I'm not feeling close enough to my dad. I want to bury a thousand questions about where I'm going to school and why my mom won't tell me. But it's the middle of the day and mom is home so I'll never get away with it.

So I do the weird thing I do whenever I'm not feeling close enough to my dad. I shut myself in my room, plug in my headphones, sit at my desk, and open the internet. I type Jorge Francisco Costa.

I click on the profile. It's on a Portuguese social media site. I found it right after Adam left.

A bearded Portuguese man smiles back at me.

It's pretty stupid, but I like to imagine that he's my dad in another dimension. That my dad looked like him and smiled like him and would have smiled at me exactly like this Jorge Costa smiles on my computer screen.

When I first tried to Google him, I found lots of Jorge Costas in Lisbon, Portugal. Pages and pages of them. Some were dead but most were alive. Some were famous. Some were old and some were young.

I found this profile. Jorge Costa, Lisbon, Portugal, born in 1987 just like my dad. I stared at his face and then started to feed pieces of his profile into Google Translate. I figured out what I could. Jorge Costa is a landscaper or he works in construction or something. He's from Lisbon but it doesn't say where he lives now. He doesn't seem to have any kids or family.

The Internet Jorge Costa has skin darker than mine and

gray hair cropped short on his head. He wears wireless glasses and a gray T-shirt. He smiles a sort of half smile, like he's happy but being professional.

He looks like a dad.

"Do the dead know things?" I ask this alive Jorge Costa, pretending he's my dad. "Do you know where I'm going to school?"

Jorge Costa just smiles at me. I let him smile at me for a long time.

But the questions are still swimming in my brain. I need more than a smile from my fake internet dad. I need answers.

I open Google. I think for a long time about what to type. What could the internet teach me about my mom?

I try **My mom is making me transfer schools.** A bunch of results pop up. I read through a few of them. Lots and lots of kids have to transfer schools, I realize. Lots of them are asking for advice on how to convince their parents not to move or not to switch schools or for advice on how to make friends at a new school. At first I feel a little less alone, but then I realize these kids aren't like me: they all seem to know what school they're going to.

I try **I don't know what school I'm going to.** The first thing that pops up is an article titled **Ten Things to Consider When Choosing the Best College for You.** All the rest of the results are about college too.

I try **My mom won't tell me where I'm going to school.** Nothing.

So I delete where I'm going to school and replace it with anything.

It's so weird to see those words all spelled out and bolded.

My mom won't tell me anything.

I shut my eyes tight. I click enter.

After a second I open them.

Advice boards pop up again. My eyes go wide at the results. Half sentences in blue font fill the screen. I want to click on all of them.

I've never met my dad and my mom won't tell me anything.

I have no idea who my father is and my mom refuses to tell me who.

My dad left. My mom won't tell me where he is.

I open one up and read about a girl whose last memory of her father is sledding with him when she was two. I read about her search and all the ways she's tried to get her mother to tell her where he is.

I read about a boy who says he looks black even though his mom is white. He says he's never met anyone who looks like him and it's the loneliest feeling in the world, but that he can't talk to his mom about it, because it makes her feel sad.

I read about more girls and boys and kids and I start to feel like they are with me, in my room. Like my room is filling up with kids and teenagers who are searching just like I am. Like it's filling up with the younger versions of those same teens who looked and looked for their dads, who worded and reworded questions, who understand what it's like to live with a mom like mine.

I wish I could meet them for real.

I'm so deep into a question by a boy who suspects his dad is a professional baseball player that I don't hear the doorbell until it's ringing over and over and over again.

Ding-dong.

Ding-dong.

Ding-dong.

I run down the hallway, rushing to get the door before Mom has to put her work on hold and gets annoyed with me for taking so long.

I open the door. It's Julia. Her arms are loaded up with books and papers.

"Hello!" she sings. "Are you sick? I brought you the homework."

"No," I say. "I don't need the homework."

I expect her to ask why, but instead she stares behind me and her eyes go wide.

"Whoa," she says slowly. She's looking over my shoulder. "What happened to all your furniture?"

"Oh," I say.

Before saying anything else, I turn to make sure Mom isn't behind me.

Mom isn't there.

Nothing is there.

The only thing behind us is the tiny coffee table covered

in papers and calendars and calculators and checkbooks and folders.

I breathe in a sob. Tears threaten to leak out the corners of my eyes.

The couch is gone.

The piano is gone.

nine
WHAT IF I NEVER FIND YOU?

JULIA DROPS THE BOOKS. THEY THUD thunderously just inside the front of our door.

"You're moving?" she says. She's almost yelling. "I can't believe you didn't tell me! You're moving!"

"We're moving," I say. I mean it to come out like a question but I leave off the question mark. Because how did I not see that? It must be what's happening. It explains the furniture. And the mysterious project Mom has been working on. And how Mom and I will go on living without Adam.

It will be easier for each of us to live day by day if we aren't in this house where memories of him haunt every corner.

"You're supposed to be my best friend," Julia says. She's standing in the middle of the pile of books, her shoulders slumped over. The front door is still open behind her so her shadow is cast long through the empty front hallway. "I can't believe you didn't tell me."

"We're moving," I say again.

"Where?" Julia says. "When? Why?"

I won't tell her that I don't know. She can't know that I didn't tell her I'm moving because I needed *her* to tell *me*. She's my best friend, but still. I can't let her see how little I count in this house, in my own family.

"Not that far," I say, shrugging.

I glance back to the dining room, where our black piano should be pressed up against the wall. What happened to the piano? Did she sell it or did she move it?

Wherever we go, there has to be a piano, right? Mom wouldn't take that away from me.

Unless maybe she found all the questions piled in my room.

Unless maybe she figured out about all the lies.

Julia turns and for a second I think she's going to leave. I think she's mad enough to walk out the door. I think—for a second—that I may never see her again.

Instead she shuts the front door but stays on the inside. She steps over the pile of books until she's standing next to me. Then she throws her arms around me and squeezes. Hard.

"Where is not far? Where exactly are you moving?"

I freeze. "Um . . ." I can't come up with anything fast enough.

Julia releases me. "You don't know," she whispers. It's not a question.

I feel naked. I'm so embarrassed I'm melting.

"Of course she does!" my mom says, coming into the living room. "We're moving to be closer to her grandmother."

I stare at my mother as Julia shouts, "Florida! You're moving to Florida! Florida *isn't that far?*"

I shouldn't be able to answer. I should be stuck processing everything. We're moving back to Florida. We lived there when I was first born but we haven't lived there since I was four years old.

And Mom just lied to my best friend. Mom said it like it was the easiest thing in the world.

Of course she knows where we're moving.

We're moving to Florida.

The only thing she didn't say was *duh*.

But I'm my mother's daughter. I know how to lie. I don't miss a beat. "It's not like it's another country or something."

Julia shrinks beside me. I see it happen. A minute ago she was towering over me. Now she seems normal-sized. I shrunk her. I have my mom's powers.

"We're moving on Wednesday," Mom says.

I raise my eyebrows. *That's in two days.* I want to yell it at her.

Julia yells at me instead.

"That's in two days! How could you not tell me you're moving in only two days?"

I have to pretend I already knew.

"Alma," Mom says. "You may pack one suitcase. Your big one. Why don't you girls go to your room and work on that?"

I start to walk to my room. Behind my head Julia asks, "Only one suitcase? To move to Florida? Why?"

"Don't question me, dear," Mom says.

By the time Julia comes into my room she's basically as short as I am.

I pull the big suitcase out from under my bed, open my closet, and stare.

I almost wish Julia weren't here. I want to be alone to think. I want sit down at my desk and write a list of pros and cons.

Pro: I love Nanny and PopPop.

Con: No Julia.

Pro: Maybe I won't miss Adam so much while I'm in Florida.

Con: I won't be able to look for Dad anymore. Maybe I'll never find him.

"Alma," Julia whispers harshly. I turn to look at her. She's sitting on my bed. "Do you really think you should move all the way to Florida?"

"It doesn't matter if I should," I say. "I have to."

"No," Julia answers. "Maybe we can figure something out."

"Why are you whispering?" I ask.

I take a sundress out of my closet, fold it, and put it in my suitcase. I've officially started packing to move back to Florida. This is so crazy it's making me dizzy.

"I mean, maybe you can stay," Julia says, still whispering. "Like stay with us."

My stomach is starting to turn itself inside out. It crawls closer to my throat. I don't like what Julia is getting at.

"My mom can't live with you," I say, like she's stupid. "Adam is your uncle."

Adam's name feels huge and clunky in my mouth. Saying his name out loud is like asking a question: illegal in this house.

"No," Julia says. "I mean just you. Maybe your mom can move to Florida and my parents can keep taking care of you."

I lower my eyebrows and turn all the way to look at her. Now I'm feeling angry at her for real, not faking it to try to get her to do something.

"Your parents don't take care of me," I say.

Julia falters. "Well, this summer—"

I interrupt her "You want me to leave my mom?" I ask.

"No . . . I just mean . . . your mom doesn't seem that . . . safe."

"What?" I say.

"Or you don't seem that safe with her."

"Julia," I say, rolling my eyes. "It's Florida. Not a war zone." I'm trying to shrink her again but it doesn't work.

"But . . . she hasn't been there for you all summer, you know? And before that Adam did a lot of the work of taking care of you."

"Is that what your parents say?" I demand. Because it's not true. My mom has always been my mom. There have always been rules because of my mom. There has always been food and good-night kisses and pianos because of my mom. She hasn't been easy to be around since Adam left but that's my business. Not Julia's. Not her parents.

Julia doesn't answer. She just keeps talking. Too fast now. "Your mom has been dropping you off over and over again all summer. And then she didn't even tell you you're moving. She didn't even *tell* you, Alma."

"Yes she did," I lie.

The lie doesn't make me feel better this time. Probably because Julia doesn't believe it.

"Kids need to be safe," she says. "Kids need safe grown-ups. Maybe you need a new one, at least for a while."

"My mom is safe," I say. "And it's not like people can just switch parents."

Although as soon as I say that I think about them. My dad who was my dad and then wasn't anything. Adam who was almost my dad, and then wasn't.

"Some kids do," Julia says.

I don't want to think about how either of them aren't my dad anymore. I tilt my head at her. "That's the dumbest thing I ever heard."

She gasps like I just slapped her.

"Who switches families?" I demand. "Parents disappear. Parents die. They don't get switched."

Julia looks at her toes. She's shorter now. I finally did it. It doesn't feel good though. "Mine did," she says.

"What are you talking about?" I say.

"My mom," Julia says.

I roll my eyes. "Your mom is perfect," I say.

"Not that mom," Julia says.

I lower my eyebrows. It takes me a minute to figure out what she's talking about. But then I do. She means her mom from Korea. The one who she grew inside of.

She's never talked about her before.

I didn't even know she thought about her.

And until this moment I've never thought about the fact that there's a woman walking around on the other side of the world who is also Julia's mom.

"Oh," I whisper.

"She couldn't be a safe grown-up," Julia says. "So I ended up with my now-parents. That's how they explain it. And I'm lucky because sometimes kids have to live with not-safe grown-ups for always."

"That's not the same thing," I say. Even though part of me knows I should stop talking about me. I should listen to whatever Julia is trying to tell me and be a good friend. That this is about Julia now and that she's trying to tell me something new, something huge—she still misses her mom in Korea.

Julia never really told me everything, either, I realize.

But I just found out I'm moving. I don't want to let this moment be about Julia. I keep talking.

"My mom loves me, Julia. She tells me that every night."

Julia stands up. "My mom loved me too," she says.

"Not the same way. Not like a real mom."

As soon as I say the words, I want to eat them back up. Who knows if her mom in Korea loved Julia? Who knows how she loved her? I don't know anything about her and I don't know if Julia does either.

"There's no such thing as a not-real mom!" Julia shouts.

I shrug. I'm embarrassed now. I don't know how to be her friend for this subject. It's too much bigger than either of us. "You know what I mean."

"I don't though," Julia says.

She waits for me to explain. When I don't, she keeps talking.

"I always thought you understood me," Julia says. "I thought all those times that I was helping you try to find your dad, you knew I understood."

"You couldn't understand," I say.

"But I do!" Julia says. There are tears in her eyes now. They're annoying me. I don't want them there. I'm the one moving. I should be the one who gets to cry. "My parents won't tell me anything about her. I find ways to ask but . . . nothing. I know why you need to find your dad. I get it. I'm the same. But this whole time you weren't ever thinking about me, were you?"

I stumble. I don't know what to say.

I feel selfish and guilty, but that makes me defensive.

"I was going with you to graveyard after graveyard, reading creepy headstones, getting rained on, wasting my whole summer. You never thought about my other mom in all that time? You never thought about why I knew how much you needed to do that?"

How was I supposed to know she wanted to find her Korean mom?

And why does she even want to do that when she already has the perfect mom?

She's making it seem like being adopted into a perfect family is as confusing and messed up as losing two dads in a row. Like adoption can somehow hurt as much as death and divorce.

"Just because you're adopted doesn't mean everyone has to be," I say. I hurt both of us with that sentence. She just doesn't know how it hurts me too.

Julia freezes for more than a minute. Her body is contorted, her mouth is half open in a way that should be impossible. It looks like I broke her.

"Goodbye, Alma," she says.

Then she walks out of my bedroom. I follow her down the hallway. I watch her collect her books and walk out the front door. She doesn't say anything else. I don't know how she gets home. Maybe she calls her mom. Maybe her mom was outside the whole time. I don't care how it happens. She's gone.

She just disappears.

She disappears because that's what people do. That's what everyone does.

Except my mom.

I spend every minute of the next day with my mom. I push every Julia-thought out of my brain and concentrate on being with her. It feels so good. It feels like one of the holes in my heart is starting to fill in again.

We go to the mall. We buy me two new outfits for my new school—a sundress and a shorts and tank combo. We buy me a new pair of sandals. We buy Mom a cotton skirt that flows off her big hips in just the right way.

Then we go to a pharmacy and buy cold medicine and cough medicine and ibuprofen and Pepto-Bismol and Tums. "Is somebody sick?" I ask.

"No, Alma," Mom says without looking at me.

I don't ask the follow-up question. I don't ask why we are getting so many medicines if no one is sick. I choose love over questions.

Mom insists on buying me fancy noise-canceling head-phones even though I've never asked for them. Still, I hold them close as we walk out of the store and back toward our car. My own mom is taking care of me.

After the pharmacy we go to the pizza place for lunch. Mom checks her watch and says, "We have to hurry back! Someone is coming to buy the car."

"What?" I ask, shocked. I almost ask why again, but then I switch to a safer question. "But then, how are we getting to Florida?"

Mom smiles. "Alma McArthur," she says, like she's giving me an award or something. "Tomorrow will be your first trip on an airplane."

I can't help but smile too.

I'm about to ask how we'll get around in Florida without a car when Mom reaches over and ruffles my ponytail. "I've thought of every little thing," she says. "I promise. You just try to enjoy the adventure."

I take a sip of my soda and nod. I'll do that. Or I'll try.

That night, my last night in my Adam-haunted house, my alarm goes off at 1:30 a.m., when I know my mom will be sleeping. She's back to wearing her hair in a tight bun, which I hope also means she's back to bedtimes and strict homework policies.

She's back.

I pull sneakers on with my pj's and tiptoe down the hallway and out the kitchen door. A light rain falls on my head and shoulders but I don't turn back for a raincoat. It's a warm rain and in some graveyard, somewhere in the greater Pittsburgh area, my dad is getting rained on too.

I sneak through the fences until I'm back where I first looked for him. He finds me immediately. He's the wind dancing around my head. He's the goose bumps popping up on my arms as the rain dots them. He's tugging at my heart so fast I can't help but follow him.

A soft rumbling of thunder sounds from far away.

The first time I was in this graveyard it was just like this. The middle of the night. Alone. In the rain.

I was certain I'd find him here.

So I'd searched and searched until I found the simple headstone that said JFC. The one that tricked me.

But now he's tugging me. I know it's him even if he isn't

buried here. A wind hits my back so hard all my hair flies in the direction he's tugging. I take a step that way and the next gust is so powerful, it knocks my glasses off my face.

I can see them. They're just a glint of green in the moonlight, skittering across the dark grass. So we follow my dad's tugging: my glasses first, then my hair, then the rest of me. When I bend to pick them up, my fingers touch a familiar *J*. I kneel and put them on. We're at the old headstone.

JFC

Suddenly there's an inexplicable smile on my face. My heart feels warm and safe despite my body being pummeled by rain and wind. I wonder if this is what it's like to have two parents. If having two parents always makes your heart feel warm.

It doesn't matter if it's not his headstone. It doesn't matter if this isn't actually where he's buried. My dad has been hanging out here, at this headstone with his initials, as close to me as he could be.

The wind dies down and it feels like his arms are around my shoulders as I kneel there in the grass.

"I can't believe I have to leave without the answer," I say out loud. Then I open the earth to bury the last question I'll ever bury in this graveyard.

Will you forgive me if I never find you?

ten

WHAT HAPPENS TO PEOPLE AFTER THEY DISAPPEAR?

MOM IS STRESSED AT THE AIRPORT. She's constantly digging in her purse and tugging on my arm and weaving through crowds and reading signs half out loud. She asks me if I have to go to the bathroom every time we pass one.

"This might be your last chance for a while," she keeps saying. So I keep pretending to pee.

Finally we end up in a long line inching slowly toward a big desk with lots of airline employees working behind it. It's been an hour since Mom said we have four hours so we must still have three hours, which seems like it would be plenty of time but Mom keeps checking her phone. She lifts her suitcase. Then she lifts mine. Then hers again. "This isn't more than sixty pounds?"—she points to my suitcase—"is it?"

I lower my eyebrows at her.

"They're gonna charge us through the nose if it's more than sixty pounds," she says. "Lift it. See what you think."

I lift my bag. It's heavy.

"I don't know," I say.

"Well, do you have any extra room in your carry-on?" she says. "Your backpack?"

My backpack has my computer, my tablet, a book, a sweatshirt, and my new headphones. Mom kept asking me if I needed to pack more to do on the plane but I looked it up and it's only a two-hour flight. "Yes," I say.

Then Mom squats so her entire body is ballooning over my suitcase. She lays it down, unzips it, and pulls out a handful of my underwear. "Here!" she says. "Stuff this in your backpack."

"Mom!" I say, mortified.

We're inching closer to the front of the line. Mom is squat-walking along the tiled floor of the airport, pushing my open bag with her feet and handing me things to shove in my backpack.

"Here!" she says. She hands me a two-pack of deodorant. I'm not sure if it's worse to have her sliding along the floor like that, to have my suitcase open for the entire airport to see, or to have her pulling out only the most embarrassing things.

If this were Mom-from-before-Adam-left, she would have weighed the suitcases before we arrived at the airport. She'd know exactly how many ounces underweight we ended up.

Of course, if this were before Adam left, we wouldn't be here. Mom would be at home working and I'd be in Mr. Hendricks's class making faces and giggling with Julia.

But I'm trying not to think about Julia now the same way

I'm trying not to think about Adam.

"Mom!" I say. "Stop! We're at the front."

"Oh!" she says, so loudly I'm sure even the taxi drivers out-side the airport could hear her. "Well, fingers crossed." She gives me a smile and straightens the long, flowy skirt she's wearing.

She yanks hard on the suitcase to right it and everything comes tumbling onto the floor. The rest of my underwear. My teddy bear. My books. My T-shirts and flip-flops and the dress I wore to the spring recital last year.

"MOM!" I yell.

"IDs, please?" the lady behind the counter says.

"Pick that stuff up, Alma," Mom says, as if she's not the one who spilled it all over the place.

But of course I already am. I'm picking stuff up and shov-ing it quickly into my bag. My backpack is heavy on my back. The people in line behind me are tapping their feet. My underwear is spread three or four feet in all directions. I'm rushing around trying to make sure I pick it all up and that I don't miss any and that there won't be some old man who holds a pair up in a few minutes and calls out, "These yours, little girl?" I'm so focused I almost don't hear the lady at the desk. But I do.

"So two passengers, one adult, one child, direct to Lisbon, Portugal, today," she says. "These are your seats."

I freeze. I don't think about teddy under my left arm and

the handful of underwear in my right hand. I straighten up. "Mom?" I say.

Above the woman's head is a lit-up sign that says "International Flights."

"Mom? Mom? Mom?" I say.

"That's perfect," Mom says, looking at whatever the lady is showing her. "Thank you."

"Yup, and your gate will be A5," the woman says. "Boarding starts in one hour."

"MOM!" I say.

Mom turns around. Her eyes are hard as rocks. I have no idea what she's thinking. "One minute, Alma," she says.

"I'll take your bags now."

Mom makes a motion like I'd better finish cleaning up her mess.

The guy behind me mumbles, "Jeez, lady. Help your kid with her bag."

But she doesn't. I shove in the last handful, zip it, and wheel it closer to her. Mom hoists it up. The scale reads 48.8 pounds, which means we didn't even need to shove all the extra stuff into my backpack after all.

We leave that line and stand in another one. Mom hands me a piece of paper and tells me not to lose it.

I study it. At the top it reads BOARDING PASS.

It says her name.

It says Pittsburgh, PA, to Lisbon, Portugal.

"Mom?" I say. I'm almost in tears. I don't know why this is hurting so much. I've always wanted to go to Portugal. "Mom?"

She turns to me so quickly her hair whips across my face.

"What, Alma? What is it? This is really not a good time for questions."

It's never a good time for questions.

I push past the anger and sadness and confusion to make myself keep talking. I won't leave here without any answers.

"You said we were going to see Nanny," I say.

"No," Mom says. "I said we were going to see your grandmother."

My eyebrows lower. Nanny is my grandmother.

"You assumed it was Nanny."

I'm so stunned all the words, all the questions in my brain freeze. *I have another grandmother.*

Suddenly Mom shakes her head, like she's shaking something off. A few strands of hair find their way out of her bun. She hugs me.

"You've been asking to go to Portugal since you were a little girl. I've been working all summer to surprise you . . . Of course I didn't want to tell you in the most stressful moment with your things all over the airport floor. I feel like the worst mom for letting that happen."

"You aren't the worst mom," I say, my words all muffled by her hug.

There are words I owe her. There are hugs and promises I

give to make up for the way I fail her. For the many questions I can't stop from rushing out of my lips. For the secret obsession I harbor that would make her more upset than anything in the world.

She wants to take me to Portugal. I asked to go. She's surprising me.

I have another grandmother.

All of this should be good. So why is it hurting?

"Can I borrow your phone?" I say. "After we get to the gate? I didn't get a chance to say goodbye to Julia."

"Of course, sweetie," Mom says. She hugs me quickly and plants a kiss on my head. Then we're at the front of the line and I have to take my backpack off and put it on a moving belt like they have at a grocery store. Behind me my mom is taking off her shoes. I look up at her and she looks worried. But when she catches me studying her face, she smiles.

"Here we go!" she says.

At the gate, Mom hands me her phone. Then she falls into the silver metal seat right next to me. I squeeze the phone in both my hands.

"Can I have some privacy, please?" I ask.

"Oh," she says, sounding surprised. "Sure. I'll just go to that newsstand right there." She points. It's only like ten feet away. Still basically in the gate. "I'll be able to see you but not hear you."

"OK," I say.

"Tell Julia how excited you are," Mom says. Then she sweeps away from me.

I don't dial Julia's number. I dial the one I have memorized and I mumble-beg to the universe that he'll pick up.

"Hello?" he says.

I miss his voice so much I feel like crying almost immediately.

"Hello?" he says again. He sounds different than he has this summer. There's an easiness to his voice that I think I missed even when I ran into him at Julia's house. Maybe I make him nervous.

"Adam?" I whisper.

"Alma!" he says. It sounds like joy. I want to believe it's real. But then he sounds worried. "Where are you?" he says. "That sounds like an airport."

"It is . . . I'm . . . Mom's . . . I don't have much time."

"Is your mom with you?" Adam asks. "Are you safe?"

"Yes. Yes," I say.

I breathe slowly in and out. Adam thinks I'm safe because Mom is with me. And he knows way more about Mom than Julia does.

"We're flying to Portugal," I say. "We're moving there."

There's nothing on the other line. I can hear him breathing. Finally I say, "Adam?"

"Sorry," he says. "I'm just . . . surprised. So she . . . she told you?"

"That I have a grandmother?" I say. I see Mom look up at

me. I lower my voice. "She just told me like a minute ago. Do you know about her?"

"Oh," Adam says. He clears his throat.

"What do you know about my dad? Do I have other family?" I ask. "Do you know where he's buried?"

"Give me a minute, Alma," he says. "Let me think of the right words."

"I don't have much time," I say.

"OK, ah, here goes," Adam says. "No matter what, I want you to remember three things. Got it? First, your mother loves you. She loves you more than anything. She has always and will always love you. She does everything she does because she loves you."

I don't know what to say but my throat makes a weird up-and-down noise. My mother is flying me to Portugal, which has to be because she loves me. Still my eyes get hot listening to those words. No one has ever spelled out the way my mom feels about me like that before.

"And secondly, everyone messes up sometime. No one is perfect. And third . . . Alma, you there? This one's important."

"Yeah," I manage

"Third, you can always, *always* call me. I can't answer anything right now. I can't . . . I have to leave the answers up to your mom. But . . . I'll always listen."

This is so different. This is the opposite of what he said when I caught him packing his bags. I've gone from *Call me when it gets really bad* to *Call me always*. I wish he had said that in the first place. I would have called him a long time ago. "OK," I say. "Oh, Mom's coming!"

"You have to tell her you called me," he says.

"Why?" I ask.

"Because you're calling on her phone and she'll see it on the call history."

My face gets hot. Why didn't I think of that?

"And because you love her," he adds. "Just get in the habit of telling the truth to the people you love. Always."

He doesn't say what I think he means: *You love her, but don't be like her.*

It makes me think about Julia and how I let her leave my house. Well, my old house now. It makes me think about how I let Julia disappear as soon as things started to get complicated. I am a lot like my mom.

"I love you, Alma," he says. And those words in his voice are in my memory so many times but I haven't let myself think about them in so long. Now there really are tears. They're pouring down my cheeks and into my mouth.

I was going to say yes to the Bold Idea. I didn't even have to think about it, really. That's my big secret from both Adam and my mom. But an offer like that shouldn't have disappeared so quickly. I've been missing his love so badly.

"Oh!" he says. "I forgot one more thing. So that's four. These are four important things to write down once you get on the plane, OK?"

I nod, which is stupid, but he doesn't wait for an answer.

"Have fun," he says. "Don't forget to have fun. Not every sixth grader gets to go to Europe!"

"I have to go now," I say. Mom is standing over me.

"I'm so glad you called me, Alma," he says. I hang up without saying goodbye.

Mom takes my face in her hands. "Oh, Alma," she says. She kisses my tears.

There are announcements that first class should be boarding now. There aren't as many people in the seats around me. I wonder how many announcements went on while I was on the phone. I wonder how much time went by. I wonder how long until I'm in a totally different life.

Mom puts her thumbs on my cheeks and wipes some of the tears away. "It's hard to say goodbye. I know."

I take a deep breath, remembering what Adam said. "I didn't call Julia," I say.

"I saw you talking," Mom says.

"I know," I say. "I wanted . . . I wanted to say goodbye to Adam."

It's still not the truth exactly. I wanted Adam to know where I was. I wanted to do what Julia said and make sure there was another grown-up watching out for me.

But I could never tell my mom that.

I wonder if lying to her makes me just like her. Maybe I should have told her everything. Maybe she should know about every gravestone I've read this summer.

"Oh," Mom says. Her face twitches about a thousand ways in half a second. Before she says anything, the announcer says, "Boarding rows twenty-four to thirty-eight."

Then she smiles. "That's us!" she says. She squeezes my hand. And we walk toward the gate.

eleven

WHAT WAS MOM LIKE BEFORE SHE HAD ME?

AS SOON AS WE'RE ON THE plane, I pull out my noise-canceling headphones, cross my arms, and look at the darkening sky through the window. I don't look at my mom, who is squished into the seat next to me. I'm mad at her. She's flying me to Portugal and I'm mad at her. It doesn't make any sense.

It's a long time before my mom taps me on the shoulder.

"They're serving dinner," she says. "Put down your tray."

"Oh," I say. I stretch forward and turn the little knob so that my tray falls down almost in my lap. I know that it's not the most comfortable thing in the world, especially if you're as big as my mom, but I love my airplane seat. It's so organized and well designed. Everything you need fits into two square feet of space: a chair, a cup holder, a tray, a movie screen. It's perfect.

A flight attendant drops two meals onto our trays and moves on to the next seat. I start to put my headphones back on but Mom says, "I thought maybe we could talk," so I leave them resting around my neck. We are surrounded by people but we're the only two in our little row. The *whirr whirr* of the plane engine makes it impossible to hear anything anyone else is saying. Out my window is nothing but the black night sky and the blinking green light on the end of the airplane wing. It feels like we're completely alone.

"OK," I say.

Mom shakes her salad dressing packet and puts the corner in her mouth to open it with her teeth. I unfold the foil around the rectangle of butter and start to spread it on my roll with a plastic knife.

"We'll be eating better than this in Portugal," Mom says. "Portuguese food is delicious."

Those words alone make me ache for Julia's family. Her father's fancy meals. The way her dad would analyze them the whole time we were eating.

"Cool," I say, but it comes out flat.

"Are you excited?" she asks me.

I know I should be excited. If I had known this trip were coming, I'd be so excited. Instead I'm just angry.

I think about what Adam just told me. I have to tell the truth to the people I love. So I say, "You should have told me."

It comes out shaky and nervous. I hate that I have to feel nervous with my own mother.

I'm sure she'll say something like, "You were too young for

the details. I didn't want you to worry. I just wanted you to have fun." Or something.

Instead she says, "I know."

I freeze with a bite of bread halfway to my mouth. "You do?" I say.

Mom sighs.

"Then why didn't you tell me?" I ask.

Mom takes a while to answer. She eats almost her whole salad. She takes many sips of her ginger ale. She shifts her weight around in the chair she's squished into.

I start to think maybe she's not going to answer me. Maybe that's all the talking I'm going to get.

Finally she says, "Did you know that when you were four, you had seventeen ear infections?"

"Huh?" I say. I have no idea what that has to do with anything.

"Yes," Mom says. "And I was only twenty-three. We had just moved away from Nanny and PopPop. I was all alone with a kid who kept getting ear infections. And when you were six, you needed to have your tonsils taken out."

"I remember that," I say. Days and days of ice cream in bed and Mom or Nanny showing up any time I rang a little bell. We lived in Pittsburgh by then, but Nanny came up to help.

"You got strep so many times. After all the ear infections, the antibiotics wouldn't work anymore so you needed, like, a super antibiotic. That always upset your stomach. You were home from school so much I lost job after job."

This is not quite how I remember it. The way she's saying it all, it almost feels like I'm supposed to apologize. But it wasn't my fault I kept getting sick. And isn't taking care of me what she's supposed to do?

"And then there was your PE teacher in elementary school. Do you remember him? Mr. Perkins."

I nod. "I hated him."

"He was awful to you. So awful. There was that one time you were sick and he wouldn't let you go to the nurse. He called you a baby. You were only seven."

"I remember," I say.

"So I had to storm into the school and have a meeting with the principal. Of course, schools cannot meet you at night. Teachers even refuse to call you at night. Everything about raising a kid happens during work hours. Eventually I had to change my entire profession just to be a good mother."

"I didn't know you did that," I say. I didn't know she switched from insurance to starting her own business translating for international professionals in order to be a good mother. I didn't know she had a meeting with the principal about Mr. Perkins.

This all feels like the Portugal trip. Stuff she should have told me sooner.

"Well, things got better when Adam was around," Mom says. "He was so . . . helpful. And he loved you."

Loves me.

"But you know, it wasn't his job to step up like that. And it wasn't Nanny and PopPop's job either, even though they did a lot. So the whole time I always felt this insecurity. I felt like I was teetering on a balance beam, you know? I had you so young, Alma. I was basically still a teenager. I had to be strict. I had to pull it together. You deserved a real grown-up for a parent, and I had to turn myself into one. I didn't have a choice. Of course, that made me too strict and too controlling."

She pauses. My mouth is hanging open, stunned. She *knows* she's strict and controlling.

"All I had for help and advice were Nanny and PopPop. They were all I knew about parenting and they were all I had. I had to accept all this help in order to be a good mom, but I also wasn't a good mom because I couldn't do it without help . . ." She pauses. "I'm sorry," she says. "Now this is too much for you. I don't want to make you worry."

"NO!" I say, too loudly. Maybe so loud the rest of the airplane can hear. What she's telling me doesn't answer my question. Not at all. But there's still relief in her finally telling me something. Anything.

"I know I didn't do everything right. And I'll never do everything right. It's impossible to do everything right because when you're a parent you are sometimes doing the right thing and the wrong thing at once."

"Huh?" I say.

"So you're right I should have told you sooner, Alma," she

says, barreling on. "But also, there was so much to do. And I had to get it all done. And I wasn't sure I could go through with all of this if you said you didn't want to go. But, baby girl, you need to get to Portugal. So I had to do what I had to do."

"I would have told you I wanted to go," I say.

And even though I already miss Julia and her family and Adam and Mr. Hendricks who I've never even met, and my bed, and the piles of questions in my old room, I mean it when I say that.

The flight attendant comes and takes our trash. When she's finished I put up my little tray and turn to my mom. I say it again.

"I would have told you I wanted to go."

Mom puts her hand on my cheek, soft and cushy and warm. She looks so deeply into my eyes I'm sure she's about to say something even more real than before. She's going to say something about my dad.

But she doesn't. She opens her mouth, closes it, then moves her hand.

"Let's try to get some sleep," Mom says. She pulls the blanket that's been on her lap up to her chin.

"OK," I say.

I pull on my blanket too, and put on my headphones. But I don't turn them on. I watch Mom close her eyes and shift so that her right ear is resting on the headrest and she's facing away from me. I look at her bun and her left ear and cheek for a long time.

My whole life my mom was this force. Or a source, source of hugs that came freely and information that came slowly and love that came confusingly.

Suddenly, she's more than that. She's a person.

Mom said we were flying all night but that's only half true because when we land it's 7:00 a.m. in Lisbon but it's only 2:00 a.m. in Pittsburgh, making it the middle of the night in my brain. I follow her zombie-like through line after line. We show our passports again; she answers questions about where we'll be staying; she shows them some other papers. It takes a long time but we get through customs and to the bag-conveyor belt. Except it's not moving and there aren't any bags on it.

Mom glances at the sign above our baggage carousel and says, "Oh, our bags are delayed."

I look at the same sign. It's glowing in both Portuguese and English but it still takes me a while to read it. It looks like the letters are swimming all over the place. I'm not sure why I'm having such trouble staying awake. You'd think I'd be used to it after all those middle-of-the-night graveyard trips. Maybe the bright lights are bothering my brain. Maybe it's the mess of people shifting in every direction around me. Maybe it's how unfamiliar everything is. I don't even know what to focus on.

"You look exhausted, sweetie," Mom says. "Go sit right there." She points to a row of metal chairs with thin black cushions that look about as inviting as the biggest, most pillowy king-sized bed in the world. That's how tired I am. "I'll get the bags," she adds.

As I sit on that chair my head starts bobbing with exhaustion. I don't want to fall asleep in the airport. I look around to try to keep myself awake.

I see so many kinds of people. There are a lot of people who look like me, more than I've ever seen before. But I think I was expecting everyone to look like me. There are black people and white people. There are a handful of Asian people. There are Muslim women in hijabs and Jewish men in kippahs. There are lots of people who don't look like me, but are like me in that they don't have an easy category. There are old people walking with canes or hanging on to younger people. There are lots of babies and little kids. There are people my age.

I recognize the sounds of Portuguese and Spanish and French around me from hearing my mom speak those languages when she's working. There are a few English conversations peppered in, most in thick accents. And there are languages I know I've never heard.

The world feels like it's growing outward, getting bigger around my mushy brain. I'm only in one building in one city in one country on one continent and I can see and hear so many different kinds of people.

It makes me feel like a tiny speck in the universe. Like my problem of a mom I can't trust and a dad who is gone is maybe nothing at all. Julia would love this.

Julia who will always be the best friend I ever had.

Julia who is mad at me and it's all my fault.

Julia who has no idea where I am.

I'm suddenly desperate to talk to her.

"Alma," Mom says. She's standing right in front of me, the handle to a big roll-y bag in each hand.

"Mom, I need Wi-Fi," I say.

She smiles. "We'll have Wi-Fi in the apartment," she says. "For now, let's go. It's time for you to see the hills!"

twelve
WHAT DOES IT MEAN TO BE PORTUGUESE?

IT TURNS OUT THERE'S A LOT of traffic between the airport and the hills of Lisbon. I fall asleep in the cab with my head on Mom's shoulder.

I'm not sure how long I sleep like that before Mom shakes me awake. I look at her, a little annoyed and foggy-eyed. She points to the front windshield. "Look!" she says.

And then I'm gaping. I've never seen so many colors on so many levels at once.

We're on a highway-type road, straight and open, two lanes going each way with an island of trees and benches running up the middle. The road runs right into the hills of the city. It doesn't actually look like hills. It looks like layers and layers of windows all arranged on top of and in front of and in back of each other. It's a series of rust-colored roofs sloping down toward our highway. It's pastel-colored buildings pushing up close to one another. The entire layered city is hugged by a blue, cloudless sky.

My heart is bouncing around my insides. My dad is tugging it this way and that, thunking it against my rib cage, pulling it up into my throat and dropping it again. We aren't in a graveyard but he's here. He's everywhere.

At once I don't ever want to move from this view and I also can't wait to be inside, in between the buildings, in the middle of those hills.

I'm breathless.

"That's . . ." I say. "That is . . . This is . . ."

"Lisbon," Mom finishes. I can hear the smile in her voice. "The most beautiful city in the world."

I take a break from the view to look at her.

I never knew she loved Lisbon, actually. I knew she studied here. I knew she knew Portuguese. I knew this was where my dad was from, where she met him. But I didn't know Lisbon meant something to my mom on its own, separate from my dad and from me.

Mom leans back, her eyes still on the hills in front of us. She puts her hand out to grab mine. "Things are going to be different here," she says. "Better. You'll see, Alma."

And maybe it's the warmth of her hand around mine. Maybe it's the calm confidence of her voice. Maybe it's the view of the hills in front of me and the way my dad is dancing for joy in my bloodstream. For some reason, I believe her.

Soon we are driving into the city, winding over bumpy stone streets so small I'm sure that I could not open my car door without it crashing into the wall next to me. There's almost no breaks between the buildings and they hunch over us on each side so that all I can see is this very narrow road and sky. It's like we are in a maze. A beautiful maze. The buildings are pink and beige and yellow and orange, all the pastel shades of sunsets. A few have intricate tile designs in brighter colors: blue and green and yellow.

We bump along slowly. Dad is holding my heart, squeezing periodically. Mom is holding my hand, squeezing every once in a while when she sees something extra exciting or beautiful, but not saying anything. Both of us have our eyes glued to the windows. Sometimes people who were walking have to jump into doorways so that we can keep driving. Sometimes we have to back into a side street so that another car can pass. If I weren't so tired, I'd be scared we were going to crash into a building or, worse, a person.

My brain is still woozy. It's like I'm taking in all of this color and architecture through a very thin straw.

Then suddenly we drive out into an open street and the sky bursts into a dome above us. We're driving down a steep hill and at the bottom is a shimmering bay of water backed by green hills and dotted with triangular sailboats. The sky and the water are so close in color you wouldn't be able to tell where one began and the other one ended if it weren't for the hills beyond. People are shadows against all the blue, walking in every direction. It's the most exciting thing I've ever seen.

In a blink, the driver makes another turn and the water is

invisible again. He drives up another curved road and then stops, suddenly. We're in the middle of the street. To one side is a building like all the rest. To the other is a set of stairs taller and steeper than I've ever seen.

The driver says something. I can't understand it because it's in Portuguese.

"What do you mean you can't drive us all the way there?" Mom asks, alarmed.

My own head jerks and my eyes go wide at her. But she starts talking in Portuguese.

They go back and forth, getting louder and louder. The driver keeps gesturing to the stairs next to us. Mom keeps saying "não, não, não," which is the only Portuguese word I understand in this conversation.

Translation: "No! No! No!"

The next thing I know Mom's handing him euros and we're out of the car, standing in front of the mega-staircase with backpacks on our backs and suitcases at our sides.

"Well, baby girl," Mom says. "Welcome to Lisbon. Guess this is how they do it."

"What do you mean?" I ask.

Mom doesn't say anything else. She takes two steps up the stairs and angles her body so her big feet can fit. She leans down, her blue tie-dyed skirt swishing over her sandaled feet, and pulls her suitcase up with a grunt. Then she does it again.

"Come on, Alma!" Mom says after she's about five feet above me. "This is part of the adventure."

So I start up the stairs, pulling my suitcase behind me. I'm so tired I don't know if my muscles are going to work. The sun is strong, beating down on my bare shoulders and hair. My ponytail is sticking to my neck by the time I reach the tenth stair. My nose is sweaty under my glasses, and they slide around on my face. I look up. There have to be at least one hundred stairs. I grunt and pull again.

Halfway up, Mom reaches a little landing area. I reach it right after her and she looks at the sky, panting. I lean down and try to touch my toes. My arms and legs are already cramping.

"So," Mom says, between breaths. "We're staying in the old part of the city."

"Yeah?" I say. That seems silly. The entire city feels ancient, like something out of a fairy tale or Disney movie. I can't imagine an older part.

"I forgot one thing about it," Mom says.

"Yeah?" I say again.

"No roads," she says. Then takes another step.

Slowly, slowly, we make it to the top. Sure enough, a sidewalk spreads out in three directions from the top of the stairs. A sidewalk with no street. Mom leans against the edge of the wall and breathes. After a minute she says, "This way," and takes off down one of the winding walkways.

The sidewalks are pavement, not stone, but otherwise this is exactly like the roads before it. There are buildings on either side of us, with an occasional break for a set of stairs down or up. I don't know how Mom knows where she's going.

My body follows hers. I'm so tired, I'm on autopilot.

Message Julia. Message Julia. I say the words in my head with each step. I have to do it as soon as I get there. I can't fall asleep without messaging her. I have to apologize. I have to tell her where I really am.

Suddenly, there's a blond-haired girl racing toward us. She looks about my age, maybe a little older. Her hair is braided into an intricate design on the top of her head. She's several inches taller than me. She's wearing a black skirt with a bright pattern stitched at the bottom and a yellow tank top that's falling off her shoulders. Her hands are out in front of her as if she's apologizing.

"Mercy!" she says. "Alma!"

I don't know how this girl would know my name.

Suddenly her arms are around me. I go stiff and I'm grateful that my own arms are tethered to my sides by my bags, making it impossible for me to hug her back. I'm not used to hugging strangers.

"Bem vinda a Lisboa! Eu sou a Leonor, a tua prima."

I know *Lisboa* means Lisbon. I smile and nod at her. Something about this girl looks familiar. Something about her eyes or her round nose.

"Pensei que a Flávia nos ia encontrar?" Mom says. She's not smiling.

The girl loses her smile for a second too. Then she says something else in Portuguese so fast I'm not sure my mom will catch it. But when my mom answers, she's just as fast. They talk for a while and then they stop.

After a beat, the girl looks away from my mom and toward me. Something about how she's looking at me makes my fingers itchy. I have to get on my Wi-Fi. I have to talk to Julia.

"This is the granddaughter of our landlady," Mom says. "She's going to show us our rooms."

The girl holds out her hand. "Leonor," she says. "Pleased to meet you."

I blurt, "You speak English?"

She giggles. "Just a little," she says. "Apologies. I didn't realize you haven't yet learned to speak Portuguese."

She reaches behind me and takes the handle of my suitcase. I want to object because she doesn't look that much older than me and the whole thing feels a little too friendly. But I'm too tired to make my mouth work. And she said she only knows a little English.

"You're going to enjoy Lisbon, I believe," Leonor says. "We are welcoming, happy people. Also we love foreigners." As if I couldn't tell that already from the hug, she links her arm in mine and takes a step down the path.

I freeze and then yank my arm away, maybe a little too forcefully.

I have this sticky feeling in my gut. Like when a new girl, Annette, first moved to our town a few years ago and started to hang out with my friends. I became friends with her eventually. But when she was first around, I didn't know how to adjust. How to make room for her.

I feel like that now. I don't want to link arms with this girl. I want to Skype Julia.

"Excuse me," Leonor says, her arm hanging dumbly at her side. "I didn't . . . I'm just so thrilled to have a prima . . . What's the English word? Well, a girl, my age . . . here," she says.

She starts down a path, dragging my suitcase. I trudge behind her, feeling guilty and annoyed at the same time. Mom and her suitcase walk behind me.

We get to a break in the wall and Leonor turns into it. She climbs three stairs and then disappears into a pathway so small she has to roll my suitcase sideways. Then she stops at a blue door.

"Avó says you'll be staying awhile?" Leonor says.

I shrug.

More answers I'm not worthy of knowing.

Mom looks up from her purse, where she's been looking for something. She pulls out a scrap of paper.

She looks bizarre holding a scrap of paper. Mom-from-before-Adam-left would have had everything in a nice notebook. She'd have a folder of papers we need. She'd be organized.

I think about the Mom on my airplane last night. The one who was more than just Mom. Who was a person.

I don't think too much about Mom missing Adam. I can't. I miss him too badly myself.

"This is it?" she says. "Right? Three forty-seven. That's what

I have written down here."

The outside of the building is a pale yellow, paler at the top where it reaches the sunlight. The blue door is wooden. It's split in half lengthwise so that the knob and lock are in the middle.

"You are correct. We'll go inside, to the second floor," Leonor says in perfect English. We enter a very dark hallway and climb a narrow spiral staircase slowly slowly slowly. When we reach the second floor, Leonor pauses at another door, which is also wooden and split into two. She fiddles with the handle for a while, then the door opens. First the right half, then the left.

"Ah," she says. "Here it is."

I have to shimmy sideways through the door and then pull my suitcase in after me. Mom does the same behind me. There's no space in the tiny hallway for three people, two backpacks, and two large suitcases. We follow Leonor down the hall and walk into a kitchen. There's a stove, small fridge, sink, and cabinet on one wall. Next to the sink there is a window, open. A soft breeze and birdcalls fall through it into the kitchen. There's a little table across from the fridge and a cozy two-person couch behind it.

The space is tiny, but it has more furniture in it than our old home. I've never been in an apartment like this. I've never even thought of an apartment like this. A space that has just enough space and no extra space.

No wonder Mom said only bring one suitcase.

I love it instantly.

This is how Dad grew up, I realize. In apartments like this.

I squeeze my eyes shut and imagine him here with us. If he were alive, he'd have taken me to Portugal before now. Many times before now. He'd be sitting down at the table, holding hands with Mom, spreading out a map between us and talking about everything we should see in the next few days.

If Dad were here, this would be only a familiar vacation and not a whole new life.

"And the bedrooms," Leonor says. We follow her back down the hall, past the split front door. The walls are white with a few black-and-white prints of flowers hung on them. The floors are made of pale-colored wood, uneven and squeaky as we walk.

This building is old. I wonder if it's older than every building in Pittsburgh. I wonder if it's older than every building in America. I wonder if it's just plain older than America.

"Here they are," Leonor says. There are only four doors in the entire narrow hallway. The one at the front is the kitchen with the couch in it. The one at the back is the bathroom. Then there are two side by side in the middle of the hallway. Mom walks into one; I walk into the other.

I guess this is my room. It has a double bed, which is exciting. But it's very low to the ground. It has no closet but a rack in the corner, where I can hang clothes, and a small dresser with three drawers. There are fresh flowers in the window. The blankets are white and the bedspread is pale blue. There's a picture of a beach scene hanging on the wall next to my bed.

I carefully pull my suitcase in behind me.

I feel very grown-up in this room. Or not quite. I feel ready to be grown-up enough for this room. I feel like I'm going to grow into it.

I unzip my suitcase, then turn. Leonor is leaning in the doorway, looking at me. I wonder why she's still here.

After I look at her for a second her face turns red. "Oh, I'll let you get settled."

I feel sort of bad. I follow her into the tiny hallway. Mom meets us there and three warm bodies in the tiny space make me feel like I'm going to pass out.

"Thank you," Mom says. "Please tell Flávia this place is wonderful."

"Do you have the Wi-Fi password?" I ask.

Mom elbows me.

"I mean, um," I say, "I love it too."

Why am I supposed to say that? This isn't her apartment, it's her grandmother's. And anyway, Mom is paying for it. It's not like we're guests.

"I need to contact my friend," I say. "So . . . do you have the Wi-Fi password?"

Mom sighs and goes back into her room.

"I'm sorry," Leonor says. "I'll ask avó and come back with it later."

I force myself not to sigh and roll my eyes. "OK. Thanks," I say.

I go back into my room but then Leonor calls out, "Alma?"

She's standing in my doorway. "I wanted to bring you this," she says. She holds a little white box with a string tied around it and moves it toward me. "We call them pastéis de nata. Um . . . breakfast treat? Yes. Welcome to Lisbon."

The minute the little box is in my hand I realize I'm not just exhausted. I'm hungry. Starved. "Thank you," I say.

I should say more. I should be friendly. Leonor stares at me like she wants a hug or something.

But I can't give her one.

I don't understand why she would bring me a treat.

I don't know her. I don't know anyone here.

Leonor leaves.

I walk down the hallway and sit at the kitchen table. Behind me Mom is mumbling and counting in her room, her heavy footsteps moving too quickly back and forth across the squeaky floor.

I don't want to think about her missing Adam or her missing Dad, maybe even. I don't want to think about her at all.

I have too much to think about. Too much to worry about. Where will I go to school? How will I make friends? How will I ever get used to this whole new life my mom suddenly dropped me into?

But I don't want to be worried. I'm in Portugal. I'm in Lisbon. Finally. I don't want to think about anything but how close he feels.

I focus on the birds and the breeze through the open

window. In the distance I hear church bells. I focus on those too.

I open the box and take out a tiny pastry. It looks like a tartlet, with a thin crust and a center ranging from white to golden brown. It's kind of a combination of a sugar cream pie and a mini crème brûlée.

I put it in my mouth and bite down. Sweetness rolls across my tongue, buttery and sugary and delicious. Church bells ring again. I stand and look out the window to take my second bite. I can see pastel buildings lining the narrow walkway. Laundry hangs on lines between some of the windows. The rust-colored roofs line up, uniform, topping buildings that look so different from one another. There are rolling hills full of the same sights in all directions. In the distance I see a hill topped by a castle. I take another bite.

I decide to pretend these pastries aren't from Leonor.

No, they're from my dad.

All of this is from my dad.

He once stood at a window, twelve years old, just like me, and ate pastéis de nata while the breeze played on his face and a castle loomed in his vision.

I close my eyes and let everything wash over me. I feel closer to him than ever.

thirteen

DOES ANYONE MISS YOU AS MUCH AS I DO?

MINUTES LATER I'M FINISHED WITH MY pastries and my head is down on the table in the nest of my arms. I'm so tired I don't even have the energy to walk to my new bed. I'm kicking my foot against the inside of the kitchen chair to try to make myself stay awake.

The kicking beats out a rhythm for me.

Stay-a-wake. Stay-a-wake Stay-a-wake. One kick per syllable.

I just have to hang on long enough for Leonor to get back with the Wi-Fi password. Then I can message Julia, fall into my new bed, and not move until an entire day passes.

Mom comes down the little hallway, still mumbling to herself.

I pick my head up.

She's saying something like "Turn to the right, left, stairs. ATM. Market in downtown. Map by ATM."

She looks at me. "Come on," she says. And turns.

I don't move. I don't think I can move.

Mom turns back around. "Come on," she says.

"Where are we going?" I ask. Even my words sound foggy.

Mom's got her hands in her purse again. Her lips are still moving. She's not looking at me.

"We have errands to run," she says.

I'm not sure if it's how tired I am or how far away I feel from everything I know, but I almost start crying. I can't run errands right now. I can't go back into that beautiful maze. I'm so tired I'm not even sure I'm awake anymore.

I stay calm, of course. Like I always do. For my mom.

"Errands?" I say slowly.

"We need food," Mom says. "We have none in the house. And we need to get you some things for school. Of course we need euros. I have a list of what we must accomplish today."

I try to get out of my seat, but I almost fall over.

Mom rushes to catch me.

"Oh, Alma," she says, much more slowly. "Are you sick? Or just tired?"

I'm not sick but I'm also not just tired. I'm worried. Worried that I have no details on this mysterious grandmother and no idea what life will look like here. Worried that Julia will never talk to me again.

But Mom has been clear. I'm not allowed to worry. I'm not old enough to worry.

"Tired," I say.

"Oh, honey," Mom says. She has her hands on my shoulders,

sort of holding me awake. Then she steers me around toward the hallway and front door.

"I don't think I can make it to the store," I say.

"I hear you," she says, rubbing my shoulder.

She pushes me past the front door and turns me into my new bedroom.

"Huh?" I say.

It's a question, so she doesn't answer it. But I can tell she's not going to make me run errands. She's going to change the schedule for me. This is not like Mom-from-before-Adam-left or after-Adam-left. This is a whole new Mom.

She pulls back my new bedspread. I fall into the bed. Mom sits next to me, making the entire mattress tip toward her so that I'm curled around her.

I'm a baby again. I'm so young I'm actually too young to worry. Or at least too young to have the words we use for worrying. I'm pretty sure I've always worried, even before I had any of the words for it.

Her hands go in circles on my back.

"Mom," I say with my eyes still closed. "When do I get to meet her? When do I find out more?"

"Soon," she says.

"When?" I say.

"As soon as you're ready," she says.

It takes me a long time to get the next words out through the darkness of my almost-sleep.

"I'm ready now."

"Well, right now, you're almost asleep." She takes a deep breath. "Alma," she says. "I'm very hungry. I think you're going to wake up starving. There's a little store downstairs, like a deli. I'm just going to run down there and pick up some sandwiches or something. I'll be back in ten minutes. Would that be OK? I'll lock the door and I'll . . . I'll draw a map. So you can find me if you need me. OK?"

"OK," I say.

She could do anything she wants right now as long as I'm allowed to sleep.

"You'll have a nap, we'll have a nice lunch, and then we'll go exploring. OK, sweetie?"

"OK," I mumble.

And then I'm out.

I'm in a deep sleep and almost immediately dreaming of Julia and summer days and headstones.

I'm not sure how long the knocking goes on before it wakes me up and I'm back in Portugal in my bed with flowers on my windowsill and someone pounding on my double wooden door. It's so strange that my dreams feel more real than when I wake up.

I figure Mom forgot her keys so I paw around on my new night table until I feel my glasses. I put them on but I'm still too tired to see clearly. I trudge down the hallway, bleary-eyed.

But when I open the door it's not Mom standing there.

It's an old lady.

She has dark, leathery skin and her gray hair is slicked back into a bun. She wears a black dress that's all one piece as it falls from her shoulders to just below her knees. She wears black house shoes and has no bag.

She's shorter than me. I'm looking down to meet her eyes. That makes this all feel even more dreamlike.

She looks into my face and then clutches both hands to her chest. My arms ache to mirror hers. Tears spring to the corners of her eyes and I want to reach out and catch them with my fingers because they are mine.

This woman with a high forehead and big brown eyes like a cat's. This woman with the Portuguese smile I always see on my own face.

Her mouth is hanging open and her eyes are wide. We're both frozen, staring at each other. She looks so much like me it's like I'm looking at a mirror through a time portal.

This is my grandmother. This is my dad's mother.

"Are you—" I start. I have so much to ask her. I have so much to learn.

But the woman interrupts me. "Alma!" she says in Portuguese. I mean it's my name so of course it can't just be in another language. But still, I feel like I'm hearing my real name for the first time.

I finally clutch my hands to my chest the way hers are clutched. "Yes," I say.

"Flávia," she says. She points to herself. "Avó."

My heart falls.

She speaks Portuguese. My grandmother who I'm here to meet will only speak Portuguese. Anything I learn is going to have to go through Mom's translation filter.

She points to herself again. "Flávia. Avó."

This is the woman who raised my dad. Who named him *Jorge Francisco Costa*. Who cooked his meals and ran his baths and helped him with his homework. Who brushed his hair and sang him to sleep. Who birthed him.

Who maybe misses him as much as I do.

Flávia sounds familiar. Flávia is our landlady.

Our landlady is my grandmother.

We stare at each other for what feels like five full minutes. I don't ever want to look away. I just wish we could talk.

"Mm . . ." Flávia avó is thinking and thinking. Finally she says, "Mommy?" then "Mercy?"

I understand she's asking where Mom is. At once I'm proud that I can sort of have this conversation and worried because I don't think I can tell her that my mom is out. Can I? Is she a stranger or my grandmother?

I fold my hands together and put my head against them. "Sleeping," I say.

"Ah," Flávia says. She hands me a piece of paper and points to her watch. It's two thirty. "Três horas," she says. "Sim?"

I think I understand, so I nod.

She points to the stairs as if she's going to leave. Then turns back around. "Três horas? Sim?" she says again. "Mommy aqui?" She points to the ground.

I nod. "Yes," I say.

Mom will be back by three. I realize I probably wasn't supposed to meet my grandmother without Mom.

"Vemo-nos em breve," she says. Then turns. But before she even takes a step, she turns back to me. She doesn't move or say anything, just looks and looks. I look back.

It's the most pleasant kind of torture. There is love in her eyes already. My blood is running with questions I can't ask and I can feel them running through her blood too. After all, we have the same blood.

She makes a motion with her fingers indicating I should lock the door, then she's gone.

I close the door, lock it, and lean against it, clutching the paper she handed me to my chest.

After a few minutes, I look at the paper wrinkled in my fist.

It's only a few letters written in shaky black penmanship.

wifi: X9hg770l

Julia!

I sit at the kitchen table and open my tablet to Skype her right away. But then I remember that Julia is mad at me. Instead I send an email.

Julia,

I really need to talk to you. There's so much to tell. Please don't be mad at me!

Please Skype when you can!

Alma

I hit send and then wander back toward my bedroom when the magical *do-dooo-do-dooo* of a Skype call ringing follows me down the hallway. I dive for my tablet and click on her icon.

"Alma!" Julia says, like it's been three months instead of three days since we last saw each other.

Cool relief fills my rib cage. She didn't disappear.

"Julia!" I say. I want to launch right into the news that I am living in Portugal and I just met my grandmother but I freeze.

I need to apologize.

I need to somehow say something so Julia she can talk to me about her Korean mom.

I don't know what to say.

She rescues me as usual. "I thought you'd be in school today. Your new school," she says. "I'm out sick."

"School doesn't start here yet," I say.

"Really?" Julia asks. "In Florida?"

I laugh. "I'm not in Florida!" My voice is a lie again. It sounds excited. Thrilled. I've somehow erased the worry, even for Julia. "My mom surprised me and took me to Portugal."

"To Portugal?" Julia exclaims. "Like to live?"

I nod. "Can you believe it?"

Julia purses her lips. "That's really far away," she says.

"I know!" I say. I can't stop sounding excited even though I also feel the sadness that's on Julia's face. We're so far away from each other now.

She readjusts her glasses. "Why?" she asks.

"Well, I have a grandmother!" I say. "I just met her. Her name is Flávia and . . . and . . . and oh my gosh, I have a cousin!"

"Like, on your dad's side?" Julia asks.

"Yeah," I say. "Leonor. She's my cousin. I didn't realize it because my mom introduced her as my landlady's grand-daughter . . . I've never had a cousin."

I don't really even understand the concept of cousins. You aren't sisters but you aren't friends. How do I do it?

"Alma," Julia says quietly. "I don't understand. Why did she take you there?"

I think about everything Mom said on the plane. All about the ear infections and awful Mr. Perkins. But really, none of that was an answer.

"I don't know," I admit. "Maybe to meet my grandmother."

Julia lowers her voice. "Or maybe *he's* there?" she says. "Maybe we've been looking for your dad in all the wrong graveyards?"

Her voice sends all the blood in my body rushing to my head. My head is going to explode with possibilities.

It was Nanny who told me he was buried in Pittsburgh. Mom never even confirmed it.

Why would he be buried in Pittsburgh anyway? This is where he lived until he followed us back to the States. This is where his family is.

She's right. She has to be. He's here. "You're right," I say. "I'm going to find him in Portugal."

I must looked dazed with joy because Julia says, "Must be nice."

I remember her Korean mom. I think about how if Portugal is far from Pittsburgh, Korea is even farther. I don't know what to say.

I could pretend I don't know what she means.

Last time I did that she disappeared. If I do it again, she might be gone forever.

"You'll get to search one day too, Jules," I try. "You can go to Korea and look. And not in graveyards."

"No, no, no," she cuts me off. "I shouldn't have said that. It's OK, it's fine. Everything is fine with me."

"Huh?" I say.

"I mean, you don't know that she's alive. No one knows if she's alive and no one will tell me anything about her, so we can't just say she's alive."

"I hope she's alive," I say.

Julia pauses for a moment, then says, "But whatever. The point is I'm sorry."

"*You're* sorry?" I say.

"Yeah," she says. "My mom set me straight. You were right. Our situations are different."

"Really?" I say. It's so weird. She's saying this right at the exact moment I realize how similar they are.

"Yeah," she says. "I mean, my mom reminded me. I have so much to be grateful for. I can still miss my mom in Korea but . . . I don't even know her, you know?"

I don't even know my dad either. Not really. Not more than I've made up in my head.

But I don't say anything.

"And now I have this family that's totally intact. Adoption is joyful. I have to work on remembering that. You're dealing with death and divorce and . . ."

She doesn't say *and a family that's nowhere near intact.*

"I'm just sorry," she says. "I have too much to be grateful for to go on about that other stuff."

"You're not supposed to miss your Korean mom because you have a now-mom?" I say.

That sounds like the worst rule in the world. It's worse than the No Questions Rule. It's worse than telling me nothing.

It's worse than any of my mom's rules.

Mom never said I wasn't allowed to miss Dad just because I had Adam.

"I can miss her," Julia says. "But who am I even missing?"

"I miss my dad," I say quietly.

"Of course you do!" Julia exclaims. "That's totally different. You don't know anything about him and . . . and he's gone forever . . . and . . . it's just different."

"I think I get it now, Jules," I say, almost in a whisper. "I get that it's not that different."

"But it is!" Julia insists. She squints and I can tell she's searching for the right words. For the words her mom feeds her maybe. For the words that are all words and no answers.

"I just have to remember to be grateful," she says finally.

"Grateful?" I say

"Whatever, Alma," she says. "You're not adopted so you don't get it. I'm lucky to have my parents. I have to remember that."

I lower my eyebrows. I can't tell if she's saying what she means. It doesn't sound quite right to me. Why should you have to be grateful for a family? That's like being grateful for air.

Every kid deserves a family.

fourteen
WHERE DID I GET MY MUSIC?

THE NEXT DAY, AFTER A LATE morning breakfast and some time unpacking, Mom tells me to put on my new sundress because we're having lunch at my grandmother's house. I already told her how I met Flávia avó when she came to give me the Wi-Fi password. I told her I knew she was my grandmother.

I knew she wouldn't like it that I met my grandmother without her, that I figured out by myself that she's more than a landlady—but that was OK.

I couldn't risk my mom lying to me. Not about Flávia avó. Not when my heart was on fire the minute I met her. Not when I don't have the language to fact-check.

Mom grounded me from Wi-Fi for two days for opening the door to a stranger but otherwise everything was fine.

It turns out Flávia lives in the apartment on the bottom floor of the building we live in.

"Alma," she says in the same happy voice when she sees us

standing on her welcome mat. "Mercy." Then she opens her arms but not toward me. Toward my mom. I'm shocked.

I guess somewhere deep inside I figured Flávia hated my mom.

I mean, it's my mom's fault I had to go the first twelve years of my life without her, right?

But they embrace and sway back and forth. It almost looks funny because compared to Flávia avó, my mom is a giant. Flávia starts speaking to my mother in Portuguese. They speak for a long time before my mom thinks to translate anything.

My heart is aching. It doesn't feel all magical the way it did yesterday. Today it's a familiar longing.

I already love this woman. I can tell she loves me.

I hate that we can't talk to each other. There's no way to connect.

Flávia breaks the hug with my mom and holds her arms out to me. Her eyebrows peak over her eyes like question marks. I nod. And then we hug.

She leads us through the dark hallway and into her apartment. The windows are mostly shaded by the taller buildings around us with no sign of the sunlight outside sneaking into the apartment, but I still love it. The walls are bright yellow and white with even brighter colored prints on them portraying animals playing and fruit bowls. There are fresh and dried flowers on almost every surface. Every table is covered in a lace cloth. It's very cheerful-old-lady.

Did my dad grow up in this apartment? Did he have bright

orange walls in his bedroom? Did he eat his pastéis de nata on a lace tablecloth?

Did he speak in that similar way Flávia does? Making all the vowels long and cheerful while clipping off the consonants as if they aren't very relevant?

I wish I knew what she was saying.

"Aqui!" Flávia says when we reach the kitchen. She points to her table covered in dishes and platters. I spot fish croquettes, steaks of cod fish, something that looks like burgers. I see baskets of bread and fresh pastries. I see what looks like a thousand kinds of cheeses and olives.

As I stare at the food, I'm almost crying. Flávia is looking at me so I don't let myself. It's a ridiculous amount of food and something about it is so clearly fancy, so special-occasion, in this tiny, dark apartment. It didn't strike me until this moment: Flávia has prepared for me. She has been waiting to meet me. I'm already twelve. Has she known about me since I was born? Has she been waiting my whole life to meet me?

She's my other nanny. And my entire relationship with Nanny is not about my mom. I can't let my entire relationship with Flávia be about my dad. She did all this for me.

For me.

I have to try to get to know her.

There are four chairs surrounding the table. Like the table they are dark wood but they each have a cheerful yellow cushion on them. Flávia pulls out one chair.

"Senta-te," she says.

I sigh. I can't help it. How am I supposed to get to know her if I can't understand her?

"Sit down," my mom says. And I do.

Flávia picks up my plate and begins to put vegetables on it. She adds one of the burgers and a slice of the cod and a roll from the breadbasket. I'm never going to be able to eat this much, but I'm going to try. I'll have a stomachache for a week before disappointing this woman who has been waiting for me over a decade.

She puts the plate in front of me and points to the fish. "Isto era o prata favorito do teu pai quando ele era menino."

"Pai?" I say.

I don't know anything else she said, but I know that word. *Father.*

Mom clears her throat like I'm not supposed to ask anything about him, even here. She says, "Vamos passar algumas semanas aqui em Portugal antes de falarmos muito sobre ele. OK, Flávia?"

OK, Flávia? Is she telling her not to talk about my dad too?

My grandmother looks alarmed. "Porquê?" she asks. Her voice is louder than I've ever heard it except when she's saying my name.

Mom answers in Portuguese so fast I'm shocked. More than fast, actually. It sounds emotional somehow.

Flávia's reply almost sounds like she's yelling.

They go back and forth, talking louder and faster and their hands flying over the food. They are fighting.

I don't know what else to do so I start eating. I shove a huge bite of slimy white fish into my mouth. I actually don't want to eat it. I don't usually like fish like this, all regular and fishy. But I think maybe she said it was my dad's favorite. So I should like it.

It slips over my tongue as their Portuguese slips around my ears, neither words nor fish really being ingested. I'm not sure which is making my stomach turn more.

I want to show Flávia that I'm not like my mother. That I don't show up to a new place and suddenly start to argue. That I appreciate everything she's doing for me. I manage to open my throat and force the fish down. I hold my breath so it stays there.

I'm supposed to like that fish. It was my father's favorite.

Instead I dig into the burger. It doesn't have a bun so I eat it with my knife and fork and it's delicious. Tender and fatty. I take some cheese and spread it on my bread. I eat a slice of fresh tomato. I focus on the food and ignore the words around me until my stomach is sticking out and my mouth is full and I realize they have stopped the shouting. They are both looking at me.

I want to spit the food out of my mouth. There is so much, I have to chew for a long time before I can swallow. Mom looks shocked. Flávia looks confused.

Eating seemed like the right thing to do but now I'm wondering if it was weird.

"Alma," Mom says. "Ask Flávia something about herself."

I turn to her. I try to get the words out without letting on that there is still some half-chewed burger in my mouth. "Did you grow up here, Flávia?" I say.

Mom translates.

She shakes her head. "Não, não, não," she says. She points to her chest. "Avó. Chama-me avó."

"She says call her 'avó,'" Mom translates. "It means 'grandmother.'"

But she didn't need to. I could figure that out.

"Avó," I say. It feels heavy and important.

She smiles.

I put that smile on her face. It feels so good. I need to find other ways to make her smile. I need to do it without words. We'll never get to be grandmother-granddaughter, our own little thing, if Mom is translating our every communication.

I swallow and look around frantically.

That's when I spot it. It's smaller than ours at home, and made of pale wood. It's shoved into the corner of the room. It's there.

A piano.

I stand.

"Alma," Mom says. "What are you . . ."

She trails off when she sees where I'm going. I stand behind the bench and put my fingers on the keys. They are smooth and familiar, like a piece of home underneath my flesh.

I turn. Flávia has also gotten up from the table. She's walking to right behind me. "Do you play?" I ask.

Mom starts to translate but she's already nodding.

"Can I?" I ask, pointing at the keys.

She nods again.

I sit and take a deep breath. Then I start. I play the opening notes of Bach's Minuet in G Major.

Flávia slips on the bench beside me. I lift my hands to make room for hers. She plays the next three chords.

I play the next three.

Then her.

Then me.

We play the entire song back and forth like that.

We play it again, this time me playing the right hand while she plays the left.

Then we play Beethoven's "Ode to Joy."

Then Bach's Toccata in D Minor.

We play the afternoon away, back and forth, speaking through the notes.

At some point my mom gives up on trying to translate and instead sits on Flávia's couch and listens to us talk.

I don't need my mom right now.

I don't need her answers for once.

Because I'm finally getting one. One answer after a million questions.

I finally know where I get my music.

fifteen
WHERE CAN I LOOK FOR YOU NOW?

MOM WAKES ME BY BOUNCING MY mattress over and over again the next morning. We went to bed early but I still have to shake my head back and forth, back and forth, back and forth before the words Mom is saying can sink into my brain.

"Get up, Alma. Leonor will be here any minute."

I pick my head up and the room around me spins. The sun is up and slipping hesitantly through my window. It's early. My head crashes back into the pillow again.

Mom is already dressed in a gray pantsuit even though she's working from home here the same way she did in Pittsburgh. Her hair is washed and combed and bun-ed.

"Leonor?" I say. "Why?"

"Alma," Mom says. "Get up."

I roll over so my head is buried in the pillow. "Why is she coming?" I say.

Something about Leonor makes me embarrassed and

annoyed at the same time. She wants to be my cousin. I understand that. She is my cousin whether I like it or not. I just don't know how to do this cousin-thing. I've never had a cousin, but from watching Julia with hers sometimes I know that the point of cousins is that you get to know them your entire life. Leonor and I will never have that. I don't know how to work around it.

"She's taking you to your school," Mom says.

"School?" I say. My eyes fly open. "School starts today?"

"No," Mom says. "It starts next week. But Leonor says all the kids go in today to sign up for clubs and catch up on their summers or something. It's tradition or something."

"I can't catch up on summer," I say. "I don't speak Portuguese."

Mom rolls her eyes like I'm being ridiculous. "It's an English school, Alma," she says. "You think I'm going to put you in a school where they don't speak English? You wouldn't learn anything."

"I don't want to sign up for clubs," I say. "And I won't have anyone to talk to about my summer. I don't know anyone."

Mom leans over the bed and pulls all the covers off me so I'm suddenly freezing. "You're going," she says.

I sit up so fast I almost knock my head right into Mom's.

"Mom!" I shout. "You have to stop telling me these things right before they happen! You have to give me some warning."

I don't know why I say it. Why I choose to argue now. It never works.

She turns, throws a towel onto my bed, and says, "I tell you things when I think you're ready to know them. If I told you you'd be going to school today, you'd have been worried about it all day yesterday instead of focusing on your grandmother and the piano."

I hate when she shuts me up like this. It makes me feel insignificant, tiny, worthless. I watch her walk out of my room, willing myself to yell at her back. But I don't.

About an hour later, Leonor and I walk through the winding streets of Lisbon. The sky is blue and the streets are bright so the morning sun must be shining although I can't see it because of all the buildings. The weather is perfect for the T-shirt and skirt I have on. We weave in and out of alleys, around tight corners. We pass tiny shops selling coffee and candy, little bakeries that smell delicious, lots of people hanging laundry or heading to work like it's totally normal to live and eat and work and do laundry in a fairy-tale village.

Leonor is trying to talk to me but we keep having to walk single file in the narrow streets to avoid a crowd of tourists or a car driving by.

She barely said one word to my mother when she came to our apartment to get me. Now, the minute we're on the sidewalk, she won't stop talking.

"It's fortunate that I attend the international school, isn't it?" Leonor says. "So that we can travel together in the mornings?"

She told me that she spoke a little English, but really her English is better than mine.

"Yes," I say. Then stop. I should say more, but I can't. I'm too nervous about all this change.

I think my mother is wrong. Yes, I would have worried about all of this last night. But I think maybe if I'd been able to worry a little bit last night, I'd be less worried now.

"When does school start?" I ask Leonor.

"Tuesday," she says.

"What day is it?" I ask. It seems like a reasonable question until it comes out of my mouth.

Leonor turns back to look at me, her eyebrows knitted. "Saturday," she says.

My face burns. I feel stupid already.

We turn a corner and the sky opens up in front of us. We're on a crowded street that slopes steeply down into the bay I saw when we were first driving in this city. Suddenly the maze is broken open and the world of possibilities floods in on me again.

Leonor stops walking in what feels like the middle of the sidewalk. There's a crowd gathered at the same spot. There is traffic stopped bumper-to-bumper in the street. There are two metal rods running through the middle of the street.

"This is the trolley stop," Leonor explains. "We'll take this trolley each morning. It drops us off about a ten-minute walk from school. It's not bad except during the rainy season." She smiles at me. "It will be nice to have a companion with whom to travel to school each day."

My stomach turns again and I suddenly want to be back in Pittsburgh with Julia. I don't think I want to travel with Leonor and her perfect English and her grown-up way of understanding trollies and her city. I don't think I want to see her every day. But I wouldn't be able to get to the school without her.

"Did you notice my braid?" Leonor asks, turning so I can see the back of her head. She has what looks like a double braid. A loose, wide French braid going down the back of her head with a tight fishtail on top.

"Wow," I say. "How did you do that?" I try to sound like I mean it.

"I've been using YouTube tutorials. I can do yours sometime if you'd like."

I shrug and too much time goes by and she looks at me so finally I say, "Cool." I manage to keep myself from laughing at the thought of Leonor watching YouTube. She's so formal and old-fashioned it seems like she's from a different century. She's using YouTube to create formal and old-fashioned braids on her head.

I don't usually think twice about my hair. I sometimes forget to brush it.

This is not someone I would have been friends with back home.

In Portugal, I don't think I get a choice who my friends are. Within two minutes, a yellow trolley comes cranking slowly up the hill. It's so crowded I'm sure we'll never get on, but people pour out of it on all sides when the folding front door opens, and Leonor manages to squeeze through two old ladies with shopping bags. "Come on then," she says.

I manage to get on it too.

It's exactly like a trolley would look. Bright yellow painted over brown wood, the paint chipping at parts. Inside there are two rows of benches lining the sides and the windows are open to the street. In the back where you'd think there are doors there are actually just empty spaces. It reminds me of something I'd see on Saturday morning cartoons.

The trolley squeaks as it moves along within the traffic of the cars. Leonor and I are standing in the middle of the aisle, holding on to the little handles that hang from the ceiling and swaying back and forth with each stop. I can't see out any of the windows. I wonder if my dad took a trolley to school. I close my eyes and feel for him tugging at my heart.

We wind around a traffic circle and then back and forth up what feels like a mountain. The crowd thins more and more at each stop and eventually I can see. The buildings are layered thick on both sides, no yards. Barely any grass. Definitely no graveyards. I don't even know where I'd look for a graveyard in this maze of a city. It all looks so different from my old neighborhood, with its sprawling lawns and vinyl-sided houses.

We start our way down the other side of the mountain. I can see out the window for just a few minutes before Leonor says, "This is us!" and bounces out of the trolley.

I follow her and we're on a real street, a paved road with sidewalks. It doesn't even look like Lisbon anymore. There's a park and a house with an actual yard. The buildings are still close together and the sidewalk is made of gray and white pebbles. It has cracks and roots growing into it. It doesn't look exactly like America. But more familiar somehow. The suburbs version of Portugal.

As I follow Leonor down the sidewalk, she chats constantly about her school. She talks about the teachers I'll have for maths and literature and history. I don't tell her that at home we call it math and Language Arts and social studies.

"Wait until you meet the Portuguese teacher," Leonor says. "She's fantastic!"

"Portuguese teacher?" I say. "Mom said this was an English school."

"Most of our classes are in English," Leonor says. "But of course we must learn Portuguese too. They don't want us to forget our Portuguese."

I stumble on the sidewalk. I don't have any Portuguese to forget. I'm going to look so stupid.

Leonor reaches out as if she wants to link arms with me again but I take a step away. I hate myself the moment I do it. But it doesn't matter for long, because as soon as we arrive at the school's campus, girls start running up to her. They hug and giggle and kiss on the cheek and fawn over her braid. They speak in Portuguese while I stand there.

The school looks like a school. It's not like my school at home, but I think I would recognize it as a school even if I didn't know what it was. It has a high wall on one side and woods on the other. The building is made of orange and white material that looks sort of like clay. On the other side of the fence are two flagpoles. One flies the Portuguese flag, the other the British flag.

While I study this, Leonor gossips in Portuguese. The girls around her touch one another and smile smiles that make me ache for Julia.

"Esta é a minha prima, Alma. Ela irá frequentar a nossa escola este ano," Leonor says, suddenly gesturing to me. "Ela é dos Estados Unidos."

The blond girl she was arm in arm with steps away from her, toward me, and says, "You'll be joining our school, then? How exciting!" She speaks perfect English too, but differently than Leonor. She has a British accent. It's like she wasn't speaking Portuguese a minute ago.

I'm so surprised by it I forget to respond for a few seconds. "Yes," I say. "I guess so."

I'm dizzy. There are too many new things. Too many surprises. No one is explaining anything to me.

"Come on then!" Leonor says, walking toward the side of the building. All the girls follow her, giggling. After a few seconds, so do I.

We sit on the sidelines and watch as a crowd of boys plays soccer in the yard next to the school. Leonor puts a winding braid in some other girl's hair. The girls slip in and out of Portuguese and English as if it's totally normal for a group of barely-even-teenagers to all speak two languages. It's sort of like they keep forgetting that I'm there and dive into Portuguese, then one of them says, "English!" looks at me and says, "Sorry, English." And they speak English again.

It doesn't matter though. I'm not saying anything anyway.

I'm thinking that even without the language barrier I'd probably never fit in here.

These girls—their braids and multiple languages—I don't think we can have anything in common. There's no way they'd be OK with how weird I am. There's no way they'd hunt for graveyards with me.

I'm hating them all for not being Julia.

After a while, one of the boys throws the soccer ball to Leonor and then all the boys run off in different directions as if a bell has rung. They're speaking Portuguese of course, so I don't know what scattered them.

Leonor stands. "Come on!" she says.

She drops the ball and kicks it in a beautiful arc. It lands right in the middle of where the boys were just playing. I raise my eyebrows at her. Leonor knows how to play soccer?

The girls all run toward the ball in the grass and I follow. Maybe we do have something in common. I've never been so grateful for all the late-night soccer-watching with Adam. And for the lessons he was always signing me up for. It's Adam to the rescue once again, even though he feels farther away than ever now that I'm on the other side of the world.

We don't play a real game. We just dribble and pass the ball around for a while. Still, it's nice to be able to keep up, to participate, to pretend like I fit in.

But the girls make me miss Julia. Soccer makes me miss Adam. Am I going to be missing home for the rest of my life?

The missing feels small, like a rodent nibbling on the side of my heart. A pain that is somehow both small and significant. And familiar.

Missing has always felt like this.

And there's someone I've always been missing.

I have to find his graveyard. I know it's here, somewhere.

That's what will make this all worth it.

After a few hours Leonor and I shed the giggling girls and walk away from the school.

"Do you think you will enjoy your new school?" Leonor asks in that overly formal and friendly way.

She kicks the ball to me. We don't walk the same way we came; we're walking through the woods behind the school. I guess the ball belongs to Leonor or something because it seems like we're taking it back on the trolley.

"I don't know yet," I say. I don't bother to point out that I didn't even see the inside. I'm still not sure what today was about. I kick it back to her.

"I understand," Leonor says. "I'll do my best to make sure you are seamlessly acquainted with the institution."

"Thanks," I say. But I don't know how she can do that since I don't even speak the language.

We continue through the woods and then emerge into a different Portuguese-suburbs street. Across from us is a big stone wall, high over my head. Nothing looks familiar.

"We catch the trolley home on a different stop," Leonor says as if she's reading my mind.

We cross the street and I dribble the ball along the concrete wall. My hearts starts to rush. Then it tugs. Something tugs so hard on it, I bump right into the wall.

The wall curves inward and opens into a high white arch with a cross at the top. Beneath it are black gates, open and welcoming.

"What is this?" I ask Leonor, pointing at the wall. "What's on the other side?"

"Oh," she says. She makes a face. "I'm afraid it's rather unpleasant."

My heart tugs again. "Unpleasant?" I say.

Then I freeze. I see it for myself.

Beyond the gates is the most breathtaking thing I've ever seen.

It's a graveyard. It has to be. Except instead of rows of headstones sticking up out of the grass, I see a spiderweb of little alleyways each lined with tiny houses. I know they are graves. Graves shaped like houses. They're made of the same white stone a regular headstone would be, except they're shaped like entire houses. Most are tiny, like only one room could fit inside. But some are bigger and look like they could have many rooms and multiple floors. The one closest to me is made of off-white stone. It has two columns next to the black front door. It's a grave with a front door. There are steps leading to the front door, almost like a tiny porch. There's a plant hanging next to the door too. It looks so inviting. It's what was missing from that JFC headstone. It's what was missing from every grave I visited this summer.

Similar grave-houses line the main street and fill up all the alleyways. They are slightly different in shape and size and color and texture and details but they are all so much more than a headstone.

It's a neighborhood graveyard.

It's a graveyard for dead people who have alive people who want to pretend they are not dead.

My heart pounds uncontrollably. I have to get inside.

I look down at my feet. The soccer ball is wedged between them. This is the most important goal of my life and I have to make it look like an accident.

I move my left foot as if I'm going to kick the ball to Leonor who is just a few feet ahead of me, walking past the most remarkable graveyard to get to the trolley like a good girl would.

At the last second I act like my foot slips and instead send the soccer ball in a perfect line drive right through the black gates.

"Whoops!" I shout. "I'll get it."

Before Leonor can say anything I rush into the gates.

I freeze again.

My heart is tugging me to the left and I ache to follow. They are everywhere. Tiny little stone houses. They each have a front step or even a full front stoop and a door. The doors are black and blue and red and green but all the stones are all shades between pure white and almost yellow or almost gray. The only thing that makes me certain they aren't actual houses is that they have no windows. Some have glass with fancy etched patterns covering bits of the white stone where a window may be if it really were a house. Some have hanging plants. Some have little flags outside. Some have doorbells. At the end of this main road is an enormous structure. It could be a three-bedroom house. Instead it's a tomb.

This is it.

This is how we should be treating the dead people we love.

We shouldn't just bury them under a tiny plaque with their initials.

We shouldn't shove them somewhere that most the world can forget about.

We should build them a house so they know they are loved. We should give them doorbells so they know they have visitors. We should hang plants for them because they can't do it themselves anymore.

My dad has to be here.

My dad has to be this loved.

He has to be this honored.

I love him.

I love him more than anyone.

In the distance I see two alive people. Men who are bent over in front of the biggest grave-house. They're planting a garden or something. One of them straightens out and puts his big hand over his eyes as if he's trying to see something in the sunlight.

I think he's looking at me.

I should move. I should walk away. But I can't.

I'm frozen there when I feel cold fingers tap my arm. I jump about five feet in the air.

"I know," Leonor whispers. "It's creepy here, huh?" She picks up the ball and walks out the gate. "Come on, cousin!" she calls.

I pause before I run to catch up with her. I don't have a choice.

But I leave my heart behind. I leave my heart at the gate of that graveyard right where my dad can get it.

I have to get back here.

Alone.

sixteen
WHAT WOULD I DO WITHOUT NANNY?

ALL THAT NIGHT I FEEL CLOSER to finding my dad than I ever have. It makes me think about how long I've been searching for him. It makes me think about how young I was when I first learned about his death, when I first yearned for a dad of my own.

I was four years old and sitting at Nanny's kitchen table.

Mom was on the phone in the next room. PopPop was just coming in from outside, mud all over his boots.

I got up and opened the kitchen drawer closest to the table. Nanny kept an entire drawer full of crayons, like crayons were as important as forks and bowls and ingredients. I loved that about her house.

"Jeez, Dad," Mom said to PopPop. "We all walk around in our socks. You have to take off your wet boots before you walk all over the place."

I stood still at the crayon drawer, two purples in one

hand, the other hand hanging on to the drawer handle. "Dad?" I said to Nanny. I'd always thought his name was PopPop.

"Last time I checked this was my house, sweetheart," PopPop said. He walked into the kitchen in his boots. Tiny puddles stuck to the floor wherever he stepped. He called Mom *sweetheart* but his voice didn't sound nice.

"Why did Mommy call you *Dad*?" I asked him.

He had his back to me, hunting in the refrigerator.

"Because I'm her father," he said. "Or so Nanny tells me."

"Oh, shush," Nanny said, swatting at PopPop's arm with a dish towel. "And Mercy's right. Take off your boots before you walk all over the living room and kitchen."

PopPop sighed and sat down at the table where I'd been sitting. He started to unlace his boots.

I walked over and put my crayons in front of him. "I didn't know Mommy had a dad," I said.

Kids at preschool had dads. I'd see them every once in a while. Kids on TV had dads. They showed up all the time.

"Well, everybody does, dear," PopPop said, not looking up from his laces.

My nose wrinkled. That was confusing.

I didn't say anything right away because PopPop looked up so suddenly. He looked at Nanny and froze. I looked at Nanny. She was looking through the doorway at Mom. She was also frozen. I looked at Mom. She was looking back through the doorway at me. She was also frozen.

I had frozen my family.

"I don't have a dad," I said finally.

"You do," PopPop said slowly. "Everyone has a father."

He had one boot on and one boot off but he still pulled me into his lap.

"But since yours isn't around, I'll fill in, OK?"

Usually I settled into PopPop's lap like it was the coziest chair in front of the warmest fireplace. Usually his hugs were second best only to Mom's. But I wasn't quite ready to settle in yet.

"Where is he?" I asked. "My father?"

I was looking at PopPop. He was frozen again. I followed his eyes to Nanny and her eyes to Mom and her eyes back to me.

Finally Nanny said, "He's passed on, sweet girl. He passed away."

They moved, the grown-ups, but just a little, like they went from frozen to slow motion.

"Mom?" my mom said to Nanny.

"We have to tell her, dear," Nanny said. "We have to tell her this."

"Where?" I said. "Where did he pass to?"

Nanny came to sit at the other chair at the table. She took my hand.

"Passed away means he's gone, Alma. It means he's . . . he's dead," she said.

I sort of knew what dead meant. I'd seen Jimmy from

school squish an ant on the sidewalk at recess. I'd heard about Cathy's funeral for her hamster. I thought I knew what dead meant. But it didn't seem possible. That there was this whole person and then there wasn't.

"But where is he?" I asked.

"He's in heav—" Nanny started, but Mom finally spoke.

"Mom," she said. "No."

Nanny thought for a minute. Finally she said, "He's in a graveyard, Alma. His body gave up. So his family honored him and put him in a graveyard."

I asked a lot of questions about that graveyard.

Nanny and PopPop stayed stiff and slow motioned. They fidgeted a lot. Mom never said another word.

That night I laid my dolls out in neat rows in my room. I took white undershirts out of my drawers and put them at their head to look like headstones. I told them they were with my dad.

My mom came to my door and said, "Alma, what are you doing?"

I shrugged. "Playing graveyard," I said.

Mom shook her head. "No," she said. "That's not a nice game."

She started picking up the T-shirts.

"Hey!" I yelled.

"Alma, no!" Mom said. "This is a bad game."

The way she said *bad* made me feel guilty. I hated upsetting my mom.

"Anyway," she said. "It's time for bed. Pick out some pj's, please."

But I didn't move right away. I stared at her long and hard as she folded my T-shirt. I stared and stared.

I thought about everything that Nanny and PopPop had said.

I thought about how glad I was that they'd been there to tell me.

Because even as a tiny four-year-old watching my mom fold up my tiny undershirts I knew. I knew that if it weren't for Nanny and PopPop, my mom would never tell me anything.

seventeen
HOW FAR AWAY IS HOME?

MONDAY NIGHT. ONCE I'M SHOWERED AND in my pajamas, after my mom comes in and rubs my back and tells me how proud she is of me and the way I'm handling all of this change, I sit down on my bed and imagine Julia is there. It's the last day of summer, for real this time. Tomorrow I go to school.

The last time I thought it was the night before school I felt lonely because I was missing my mother.

This time I feel lonely because I'm missing Julia. It'd be so different if she were able to go to school with me tomorrow, even here, in Portugal. If I had her to laugh with and share homework notes with and make other friends with.

No one wants a friend obsessed with graveyards and a dead person. No one except Julia.

I decide to try to Skype her again even though I know she won't answer. It's four o'clock in the afternoon in Pittsburgh. She's at soccer practice.

It rings and rings. No answer.

I take off my glasses, climb into my low-to-the-ground double bed, and go to sleep.

In the middle of the night, I'm suddenly awake.

My tablet is beeping next to my bed.

I jump to catch it before it wakes my mom up. Julia's picture is lighting up the screen. I hit the green circle and whisper, "Hi!"

"Hi!" she says at normal volume. "I'm so glad you picked up!"

I can hear the sounds of her house behind her. Her mom yelling at her brother for tracking mud into the house. Her dad watching TV. It's so weird that it's evening for her and it's night for me. It's like we aren't in the same world.

"Mr. Hendricks is the worst," she's saying. "He gave us so much homework this weekend, you wouldn't believe it. You're lucky you don't have to have him," Julia says.

Part of me aches for this. For whining with her about too much homework. For the normalcy of my old life. But I know if I were with her I'd never even realize how great it was. She'd be whining about homework and I'd be on her computer plotting some way to get to another graveyard.

I listen for sounds in my own world. Through the paper-thin walls I can hear my mother snoring. It's safe to talk.

"You'll never believe it!" I whisper. "I found the most incredible graveyard." I launch into a description of the little streets and the houses made of white stone and the front porches. The little bit I saw.

"Google Image it," I say. "You'll see what I mean."

Julia has been quiet ever since I started talking about the graveyard but the screen freezes and I know she's Googling it.

"Whoa!" she whispers. "That's so creepy."

Her face is back on the screen. "Isn't it amazing?" I say.

"It's—" she starts, but I don't let her finish.

"I couldn't really explore. Because my cousin was with me."

"Your cousin?" Julia says.

"Yeah," I say. "The one I told you about. Leonor. She lives with my grandmother, I guess."

"Back up, back up!" Julia says. "You went out with your cousin? You went to your grandmother's place?"

"Yeah, she actually lives right downstairs," I say. "I had lunch there the other day. We played the piano together."

"What?" Julia says. I watch her deflate. "How could you not tell me that?"

"I don't know," I say. "Avó—that's like *grandma* in Portuguese—doesn't even speak English. Mom had to translate so who knows what she's saying."

"Oh," Julia says. "What about your cousin?"

"What do you mean?" I ask.

"Like, tell me about her. How old is she? What's she like?"

I pause. I have a cousin. I have a cousin on my dad's side and I finally met her after all this time. I wish it felt better but maybe it just reminds me that I'll never have my dad.

"I don't know how to do it, Jules," I say finally. "I never had this sort of family, you know? Cousins and aunts and uncles.

My world was always so small. Leonor really wants me to like her but . . ."

"Well, she must," Julia says. "She took you to a graveyard."

"No, no, no," I say. She's not understanding anything.

I shift on the bed so I'm lying on my belly with the tablet propped up in front of me. It's almost like Julia and I are lying face-to-face. This is a much better way to get ready for the first day of school.

"She didn't have to take me to it. That's the best part," I say. "It's right near my new school. Leonor took me there the other day for some sort of orientation and on the way back to the trolley—"

"Excuse me!" Julia interrupts, way too loudly. "You went to school? On a trolley? . . . I'm missing the most important parts!"

I'm not answering Julia because I'm listening for snores. I turn my head to focus on the wall.

Snore, please. Snore.

I have to tell Julia the rest about the graveyard. If Mom wakes up she's going to come in here and make me hang up. No electronics after bedtime is one of her rules. She'll take my tablet for a week.

"Alma?" Julia says. "You aren't even looking at me."

"Sorry," I whisper back. "My mom's asleep. She probably wouldn't want me talking right now."

"Oh, OK," Julia says. "I'll whisper."

"Thanks," I say.

It doesn't feel right, meeting all this family. I thought I would like it more than I do. I thought it would fill in a little bit where my dad is missing inside me. I thought it would fill in the hurt just a little.

But instead I feel the gaps of him widening. Leonor is only interested in me because of a dead man I don't know anything about. Avó is only feeding me because of the same dead man.

I don't know how to focus on the other things. I only know how to focus on my dad.

I pause. I hope I've paused long enough before I keep talking. "But wouldn't it be amazing if my dad is buried in that graveyard. It's the most beautiful graveyard in the world."

"I don't know, Alma."

I'm smiling huge but Julia doesn't smile back. She studies her lap or her shoes or something beneath the screen of my iPad, something back in her world where things are solid and make sense.

"And it must mean something that it's next to my new school, right? Like he's finally leading me to him, right?"

"I don't know, Alma," Julia says again.

"What do you mean you don't know?" I say. "This could be it. It could be the end of the search!"

She's been to so many graveyards with me. She's done so much searching. I need her to get excited. I need her on my team.

But she sighs. "I guess so," she says. "Will you tell me about the school?"

"Are you upset because you won't be there when I finally find him?" I try.

"No," she says. "I'm not upset. Tell me about your school."

"Are you mad that I don't have to do all this homework from Mr. Hendricks with you? Or that I got to travel to another country?"

"No!" she says.

"Are you—"

"Alma!" she says. "I'm not upset. I'm . . . I just can't think about missing moms and dads all the time. Sometimes I want to hear about school and kids and cousins and normal stuff."

I lower my eyebrows. "I didn't say anything about missing moms," I say. I never have. My mom has been a lot of things, but never missing.

Julia shakes her head. I can't tell if it's my tablet or the lighting or if her eyes are getting a little red. "I know," she says. "Can we please just talk about the normal stuff for a minute? Anything except graveyards?"

"OK," I say slowly. Then I remember. Julia is my friend, not my cousin. I know how to be good to her. "Wait. Jules, when I talk about my dad and graveyards, does that make your miss your mom from Korea? Is that why you're angry?"

"I'm not angry!" Julia shouts.

"Julia!" Her mom's voice pops out of the background. "Who are you talking to for so long?"

"Just Alma," Julia calls back. She makes her voice cheerful and happy. It's so instant it's like a magic trick.

"Alma?" her mom says. She appears on the screen behind Julia.

"Alma, how are you?" her mom asks.

"Hi, I'm fine," I say.

"She has her first day of school tomorrow," Julia says.

Julia's mom checks her watch. "Alma," she says. "It's one thirty in the morning in Lisbon. What are you doing on your tablet?"

My face burns. She sounds just like my own mom. I don't need her to sound like that anymore though. My mom is mom-ing me again.

"I just wanted to talk to Julia," I say.

"You girls hang up now," she says.

But we can't. I know we can't. I have to find out what Julia is feeling right now, what she was trying to tell me about her first mom.

"You need some sleep before school tomorrow," Julia's mom says. And that might be true. But I need to get to a better conversation stopper with Julia more than I need sleep.

She tried to talk to me about her other mom one other time. And I blew it. I'm not going to blow it again.

"Five more minutes," I say.

Julia's mom looks at me like I have five heads. "Good night, Alma," she says. "We don't negotiate at one thirty in the morning."

Julia looks sad and defeated. I don't ever want to hang up with her when her face looks this broken.

"Good night," she says. And she hangs up.

My room is suddenly extra dark. I roll over and stare up into the darkness. The noises of the city pour in my open window, people partying and calling out to one another late into the night.

All their voices sound like Julia's.

Missing moms and dads.

I'm going to find my dad in the beautiful graveyard.

Then I'll have to convince Julia to let me help her find her mom.

A new day at a new school in a new city in a new country should be enough to keep my mind occupied. But I can't help thinking about the beautiful neighborhood graveyard that is only a few blocks away. The one I'll get a glimpse of on the way home today.

Leonor meets me at the bottom of our apartment building and we walk over to the trolley. I think she can tell I'm nervous because she doesn't talk too much.

Like Mom promised, the teachers all speak English most of the day and the kids are all pretty nice. Some things make me stand out: my frizzy hair that I wear down with just a headband, my backpack that I wear on both my shoulders, and the fact that the teacher, Ms. Sousa, announces that I'm from Pittsburgh in the USA. But there are kids at this school from all over the world.

The morning seems to speed by. Ms. Sousa announces

that we'll be reading *The Giver* as our class book to start the year. I already read it in fourth grade. Ms. Sousa starts us on a "review" worksheet for math. All the kids around me start dividing fractions in a way that looks completely foreign to me and Ms. Sousa stands over my desk attempting to walk me through it while I try to make my brain listen to her and stop repeating *Dad Dad Dad*.

At lunch we move to a different kind of room. It's like a big balcony lofted over the front entrance of the school. There are groups of desks pushed four together to make a little table and each of them is covered in blue tablecloths with cups and silverware laid out. It's very formal for school lunch and it makes me stop thinking about my dad for just long enough to miss the sticky and loud cafeteria that Julia and Annette and Sharice are in right now, except they aren't, because lunchtime in Lisbon is not lunchtime in Pittsburgh.

I try to focus on what's happening here. On this new school where I should be trying to make friends.

The girls and boys all arrange themselves into lines and seem to know exactly what they're doing. I panic for a quick second because I'm hungry and I don't know how to get food and I look like a fool. Then a girl comes up behind me and says, "Get on line here, get your tray, and choose a table."

She pulls my wrist so I end up behind her in line.

She turns back to me and says, "I'm Suzanne." It's then that I realize she doesn't have an accent. Or maybe she has my accent.

"I'm Alma," I say quietly.

I follow Suzanne down the lunch line until I'm carrying a heavy tray. It has a plate with pasta on one half and some sort of beef stew on the other. It has a bowl of pink soup in one corner. It has a slice of some delicious-looking white cake on the other. It's the best school lunch I've ever seen.

"Here," Suzanne says. "Sit with me."

I sit at a table with her and two other girls.

"You don't look American," one of the other girls says. She's Portuguese. I'm beginning to be able to tell by the way someone speaks.

She's also black and doesn't look how I always thought Portuguese people looked but I don't say that. I guess I thought all Portuguese people would look like me. I know now that was silly.

"Alma isn't an American name either," the other girl says. "At least I didn't think so."

"My dad is Portuguese," I say without thinking.

"Oh, that's why you're here then," Suzanne says. "He brought you back, huh?"

"Yeah," I say. Then I stop.

I could tell them my mom brought me here. I could tell them my dad is dead and it's my mission to find out where he's buried. I could try to make a new friend here at this lunch table.

But at home everyone knew my dad was dead. Here no one does. If I don't say another word, I seem like a normal girl with a Portuguese dad who loves her. I seem like the girl I've always wanted to be.

I can be that girl in this new school.

I can be that girl right now.

"My dad wanted me to get to know his country," I say. I leave it at that.

I'm turning into my mom. Just giving people the little pieces I want to share. Keeping most of my own story to myself.

After lunch I follow Suzanne and the two Portuguese girls down an unfamiliar hallway and into a different classroom. The posters on the walls are not in English. The books on the bookshelves are not in English. The music playing from the teacher's computer on the desk where she's sitting is not in English.

We sit and the teacher stands. She does not smile.

She says, "Bem-vindos de volta, alunos! Feliz primeiro dia de escola."

I try to translate in my head as much as I can.

Bem-vindos sounds like welcome.

Escola is school.

But by the time I get that far, the teacher is talking and talking and the kids around me are laughing and laughing.

I deduce that this is Portuguese class.

I deduce further that if I felt like I was behind in math, I'm never catching up in this class.

Dad Dad Dad Dad

For the next hour I stare into space and imagine my dad's grave in the neighborhood graveyard. It'll be one of the whiter houses, I think. The cleaner ones. Surely avó has been taking good care of him all of this time and now I'll go and help her on Sunday afternoons. I'll bring little hanging plants for his grave-porch and I'll clear off the mud during the rainy season. We can sing songs together, avó and I, since we won't have a piano there. We can honor Dad together.

Dad Dad Dad Dad

I'll have to find a way to visit him. I'll find a way to get away from Leonor one day after school and I'll go straight to the graveyard.

Dad Dad Dad Dad.

I'll visit him every day if I can until I know everything there is to know about him. Did he grow up here or in the south of Portugal like the rest of my family? Did he go to this school and ride this trolley?

Dad Dad Dad Dad

Is he so proud of me now, seeing me in his old city?

Dad Dad Dad Dad

I'm so far in my head that I'm a few seconds behind as everyone else stands and picks up their books and moves to the back door of the classroom.

"Alma," the teacher says, the first word I've understood in what feels like forever. "Come here."

I walk to her desk. She has a card in her hands and she's scribbling quickly.

"Take this home to your parents," she says. "I'd like to see you after school one-on-one until you can catch up a little bit. It may be a lot, but I'm thinking about several times a week. We have to work hard if you're going to learn the language."

I try to hide my smile. I'm not supposed to be excited about staying after school. But I know what this will mean.

I'll be going home on the trolley without Leonor.

I'll be able to visit Dad's grave by myself, three times a week.

Just the promise of it is enough to keep me from more than glancing at the graveyard on the way home from school.

That evening my mother makes spaghetti. The old-school kind with just plain sauce on just plain noodles with Parmesan cheese sprinkled on top. I'm so happy for something so usual, so familiar. I could almost cry.

I hand her the note. She reads it. "Would you like to learn Portuguese, Alma?" she asks.

I lower my eyebrows at her so low they almost push my glasses off my face. Seems like a question she should have asked a long time ago.

"It's just that you've never shown any interest. And if we agree to you staying after school this much, you'd have to work hard to learn the language."

"Yes," I say. "I'd like to."

"Well, OK then," Mom says. "I'll write back to the teacher and set it up."

I nod.

"I spoke with your uncle today." I freeze with a bite of spa-ghetti so close to my mouth it starts to drip on my lap.

"My uncle?" I say.

"Leonor's father," she says.

Leonor has a dad.

"Oh," I say.

"We were trying to figure out how you can meet everyone without it being too overwhelming."

"Everyone?" I say. My voice is a little shaky.

"All your aunts and uncles and cousins," Mom says. "They live all over the country."

"How many are there?" I ask.

"Lots, apparently." Mom says this like it's no big deal. Like going from having a tiny family of just Mom, Nanny, Pop-Pop, and me to a huge family that has to travel from all over an entire country just to see you should be super easy and normal.

I don't think I'm ready for this.

I'm still getting used to Leonor and avó.

I have to find my dad before I can even think about the rest of his family. How can I get used to this family if my link to them is missing?

Mom rubs my cheek. "I want you to meet your family," she says, as if she's giving me some priceless gift. Which maybe she is. But it's *my* family. She sort of owes it to me.

She's still talking. "Your uncle says you and Leonor have a

long weekend in October, sometime right around when you would have fall break at home."

This makes me think of last fall break. Of Mom taking me and Julia to a pumpkin patch. Of Julia's dad making us hot apple cider from scratch.

"So he suggested they come that weekend. To get to know you. How does that sound?"

It's a month and a half away. I can't even get my brain around the fact that I'll still be here then.

By then, I will have found his grave. I'm certain of it.

By then a lot of things will be better.

Before I can answer, Mom's cell phone starts ringing in her bedroom. She gets up to answer it and I finally take my bite of spaghetti.

Then she comes back into the kitchen. "It's for you," she says.

I jump up and skip down the hallway. Silly me not turning my tablet on so that Julia could Skype. She had to call my mom's phone.

I sail into my mom's room and plop down on her bed where the phone is facedown. I yank it close to my ear.

"Jules? You'll never believe my school lunch," I say.

"Alma," says a voice. It's not Julia's. It's a deep voice. A man's voice.

Adam.

"Sorry to disappoint you, but I'm afraid I'm not Julia," he chuckles.

My whole body breaks out in goose bumps. I sort of mumble, "It's OK," but that's not what I mean. It's better. It's wonderful.

I don't need to wait for a catastrophe to call Adam. He's calling me.

"But I want to hear about this school lunch," he says.

I grin and launch into details about the pasta and meat combo. I tell him about the trolley and about Leonor and how I have all sorts of other family I still have to meet. I tell him about playing the piano with avó. I'm surprised how much I'm talking. I tell him about every single thing except the beautiful graveyard and how certain I am that I'm about to finally find my dad. It's almost like old times, like third grade when Adam would come home from work with take-out cheeseburgers and we'd sit around the kitchen table and I'd talk-talk-talk.

But it can't be that normal because they are divorced and I'm in Portugal and Adam asked about the Bold Idea and then Adam's Bold Idea went away.

My chatter halts.

"Anything else going on, Alma-bear?" he asks.

"No," I say.

"Are you doing OK?" he asks.

"I'm good," I say. "Hey, why did you call?"

"I wanted to know about your first day of school," Adam says.

"Oh," I say.

In my head I ask him, but why didn't you want to know about anything else? Why didn't you want to know how I was back in Pittsburgh? Why didn't you want to know why I was at Julia's all the time? Why do you suddenly care about my day when for months you just disappeared?

I'm afraid to ask him any of that though. What if it makes him disappear again?

Too much time goes by, then he says, "Is it OK if I call now and then?"

"Yeah," I say. It's OK. But it's not enough.

Silence again. I can't think of anything to say because my brain is full of questions I'm too scared to ask.

Finally I say, "My dinner is getting cold."

"All right, Alma," he says. "Just remember I love you. Your mom and I, we—"

Except I hang up on him. I don't want to hear what he's going to tell me to remember. I don't want him to pretend to be some hero when all he made is a phone call.

Hearing his voice on the phone seemed so huge. But it's tiny when I remember the Bold Idea that disappeared.

eighteen
IS THIS WHEN I FINALLY FIND YOU?

IT'S THE SECOND WEEK OF SCHOOL by the time Mom and my Portuguese teacher have worked out a way for me to stay late a few days a week for extra tutoring. The schedule is a little different each week so Mom says it's up to me to keep track and let her know which days I'll be staying late. The teacher starts with the super basics like hello (*Olá*) and goodbye (*Tchau*) and how to count (*um, dios, três*) and other things I already know just from listening to my mom talk on the phone for all these years. I'm glad it's easy because I'm too distracted to pay attention.

I'm finally going home alone.

I can finally make my detour.

As soon as I get out of school, I run the whole way to the graveyard. I've been in school so long the sun is sinking low in the sky and the shadows of the trees in the woods have grown to meet one another. I can almost hear footsteps beside me.

It's almost like Julia is here with me, where she should be, helping me solve the mystery, ending all my questions.

I sprint all the way to the gates.

The pull on my heart is so strong that I've never been this sure of anything in my life. My dad is in here. In these gates.

I see a trolley coming up the hill. For a second I want to get on it. For a second I want to leave the mystery where it is.

But it's even more than that. It's that I've been searching for my dad for as long as I can remember. I've been as close to him as a living girl can be to a dead father.

What will I look for after I find him?

What will I think about once the mystery is solved?

What if I find him and I don't feel anything?

I think about going home and calling Julia and telling her I didn't go in. "You're crazy!" she'd say. "You can't choose to have missing moms and dads if you don't have to."

Instead, I step slowly inside the gate. Immediately I'm a different person. My heart is calm. My breath is even. Each mouthful of the darkening air tastes like the freshest water from the freshest stream.

It's a little chilly so I pull on my uniform red sweater. It feels like Mom's hug surrounding me.

All my life I've had one parent. And now, I'm about to have two—I'm sure of it.

I walk down the main street of the graveyard. I'm still in awe of all of this—these Houses for the Dead on either side of me, close together and sometimes touching. I reach out and stroke one house, half expecting it's going to be Dad's just because it's the first one I touched.

But when I read the letters carved above the door it says *Gloria Lopes*. A woman's name.

I wander the main big street. The graveyard is almost empty. Just a few people walking near me, taking pictures or talking in hushed voices.

There's no Jorge Costa on the main road. At the end of it is the grave version of a mansion. It looks to be three stories high and it has a porch with four front steps. The front and sides are meticulously landscaped with flowering plants and beautiful trees. I see a man working on planting something behind it. I stare at the house for a while. It looks like I could walk up the steps and knock on the front door. It looks like I could be invited in for tea and a chat. It looks like it's keeping the dead person inside while inviting the rest of the world in too. Isn't that how it should be?

My heart pulls me to the right. It's a yank and I have to follow it.

But as I turn, I see tiny alleyways that spiderweb in every direction. The graveyard goes on for so long it would take me hours to read every name on every doorway. I look at a few. No Jorge Costas.

The sun is sinking further and shadows are all around me. If I don't get home before it's dark, Mom will be freaking out. She'd ground me if she knew where I was. My heart feels heavy. Like it might fall out of my body and rest here in this graveyard until I can come back and get it.

But I have to go.

I start walking backward, looking at the graves as I go.

"I'll find you soon, Dad, I promise." I say it out loud, as quietly as I can.

Then, *SMACK*. I back right into something. Someone.

"Ahh!" I scream.

"Cousin! Cousin! I apologize! I didn't mean to startle you."

I turn. "Leonor! What are you doing here?" I spit.

In two seconds I'm so far from the calm I just felt. I can't feel my dad anywhere anymore.

"I am truly sorry," Leonor says. I walk past her and start my way toward the trolley, pretending not to listen as she keeps talking, trailing behind me. "Avó told me you were required to stay late at school for some additional language lessons and . . . and I only thought you may need some assistance finding your way home . . . . I was waiting in the front vestibule but then you left the school so quickly . . . I chased after you, but I'm afraid you are much faster than I. I followed you here to see if you needed assistance and then—"

"My mom sent you," I say over my shoulder. "Didn't she?"

"No," Leonor says. "Avó didn't send me either. I assure you it was all my idea that you may need some help navigating back home."

I turn so that we're face-to-face. I feel like I'm towering

over her even though she's several inches taller than me.

"Then listen," I say. "You can't tell them where I was. You can't tell anyone."

"OK," she says. She almost looks like she's trembling. "I will not tell your secret, Alma."

I nod once, satisfied she's not going to say anything. I soften a little. She was trying to help me. It's not her fault I'm weird and needed a minute alone in a graveyard.

"Come on," I say. "Let's go home."

Gray clouds are rolling across the blue sky, darkening the graveyard. I take a few steps, then say, "And thank you. I mean, thank you for staying late to be sure I get home. I didn't mean to yell . . . I just needed . . ."

Except when I turn Leonor isn't right behind me. She's still standing a few feet back, where she was before I started walking.

"Alma?" she says in a voice so tentative, I forget all about how annoyed I was and walk back over to her.

She bites her lip but doesn't say anything until I say, "Yeah?"

"Were you . . . did you say . . . were you . . . Did you think your dad would be here?" she asks. "My tio Jorge?"

A light bulb goes off. My eyes get wide. She could know. She could *know*.

"What do you know about him?" Leonor is saying.

"Is he not here?" I say, fast. "Do you know where he is?"

Leonor shakes her head, her eyes on her shoes. "I'm afraid no one does at the moment."

My heart stops. My face is on fire with anger. *No one* knows where he is? Does no one care about him except me?

"What?" I say, almost screaming. "What do you mean no one knows where he is?"

"The family hasn't seen him in a long time," Leonor says.

"What?" I yell. "How? He didn't even get a funeral? His family doesn't know where he's buried?" His family doesn't even love him?

I'm hysterical.

It's contagious. Leonor answers me in the same panicked tone.

"He's *dead*?" she cries. "Tio Jorge is dead? No one told me!"

They've told her less, I think. She knows even less than I do. Maybe avó does know where he's buried. Maybe she did what my mom would and kept the truth from the children.

"When did he die?" Leonor asks.

"A long time ago," I say. "When I was a baby. In Pennsylvania."

Leonor's eyes go wide.

Then she sits. She's suddenly sitting on the grass next to the stoop of a grave-mansion, despite the clouds over her head threatening to drench us.

"Leonor?" I say.

"I . . . I . . . dá-meum minuto . . . I mean, give me a minute."

I watch her sit there, swallowing big gulps of air. Finally she says, "Your mother and avó have been quite clear: I am not permitted to talk to you at all about tio Jorge. But I'm afraid I must. I must break that request."

"They said we can't talk about him?" I say, looking at her. "Why? What do you know?"

Leonor looks right in my eyes and says, "Cousin, I'm not sure how or why this happened. But your mother has a misunderstanding. Your father is not dead. He is alive."

"What?" My bag drops off my shoulder. My jaw drops to the ground. Then I laugh. Because it's impossible. It's the only thing I've ever know about him. The only speck of truth I've ever had. He's dead.

"This must be quite shocking," Leonor says. "I am befuddled for you, I believe."

"He can't be alive," I say, shaking my head. "He can't." He can't.

Every question I buried has to have gotten to him somehow. Every time I thought of him, I had to be thinking of the right person. The dead person.

"Well, it's been two years since I've seen him. But he was very much alive then. And I don't believe he was ever in Pennsylvania."

I stare at her, her words barely getting through my ears into my brain they are such nonsense.

"I'm so sorry, cousin," Leonor says.

But she's wrong. She has to be.

"Then why does my mom think he's dead?" I demand.

"I don't know. Avó tells me precious little. I don't know what she's told your mother. Tio Jorge is not easy to find. But

I have met him. I have seen him. Long ago, but much more recently than when you were first born."

"No," I say. "You can't have seen him. You're making this up. You're making fun of me."

"I wouldn't do that," Leonor says. "I promise. It's true. Your dad. He is alive."

I stare at her. Her eyes are wide. She's trying to look as honest as possible. But she's turning my world upside down. She's changing the way I'm grounded to the planet. She's erasing gravity. I'm afraid if I listen to her say it one more time, I'll disappear.

Before I know what I'm doing, I turn and run. I run fast and then faster, weaving my way between grave-houses and grave-mansions until I reach the front gate. I hear the trolley ringing and I dive onto it just as the rain erupts behind me, leaving my cousin in the cloudy graveyard where my dad must be buried.

Must be.

nineteen

WHAT?

I BURST THROUGH THE WEIRD DOUBLE doors of our tiny Lisbon apartment and it seems like all the air rushes out of my lungs, as if I'd been holding my breath the entire ride home.

"MOOOOOOM!" I scream.

I'm a mess. My bag is still in the graveyard. My glasses are crooked on my nose. My uniform shirt is half untucked, my red sweater is falling off one shoulder, and half of my hair has come sprouting out of my ponytail in all directions.

"MOOOOOOM!"

Her bedroom door slams open and she appears before me.

"Alma! Alma!" she's saying. "Are you OK?"

It's not until I see her face that I realize I can't say anything to her. Now that Adam's gone she's the only person in the world who loves me in that firework-heart way and yet I can't trust her with any of my thoughts.

If I tell her Leonor says he's alive, she'll keep me from trying to find out if he really is. And if I tell her where I've been, she won't let me go back. She'll keep her eyes on me all the time.

Still, I fall into her hug when she opens her arms for it.

"You're soaked," she says.

I didn't even realize it had started raining, but I think about my skin and yeah, she's right.

My first rain in Portugal.

I feel my back rising and falling with breaths so big I could choke on them as my mom's hand strokes and strokes my wet uniform sweater. I have to pull it together. I have to come up with something else to say.

"I—I—I—"

"Alma, honey, what's wrong?"

"I left my bag at Portuguese class," I say finally. It's almost a wail.

"Oh, sweets," Mom says. She holds me tight and rocks a little bit. "It's OK."

I freeze in her arms. Her hug is not doing its usual warming-thing. I can't believe I just lied like that, so easily. I don't want to become a liar just because my mother is one.

"I don't think I like this," she says. "I don't know about a twelve-year-old taking the trolley all by herself."

"Am I late?" I ask. I look toward the kitchen window but it's hard to tell because it's dark and raining outside.

"No," she says. "But look at you. It's too much."

I step out of the hug.

"I've been taking the school bus by myself since kindergarten."

The words are the truth but the way I say them—calm, pulled together, almost whiny—is a lie.

"There's a big difference between the school bus in a tiny suburb and the public trolley in a big, foreign city. I'm not sure what I was thinking. I'll come and pick you up tomorrow. I'll rearrange my schedule to take some calls after dinner. That way I can ride the trolley home with you."

"NO!" I say, too loudly, too jumpy.

I don't tell her that I don't have Portuguese lessons tomorrow. I need her to think that I do.

Mom cocks her head. "Are you sure you're OK?" she asks.

"Yes, just . . . All the kids take the trolley, Mom," I say, finding the words out of thin air. "I'll look like a total baby."

I don't feel this way. It was only a few weeks ago that I was standing on the bus stop at home aching for my mother to be there with me. I actually love that she would be willing to change her whole schedule just to ride a trolley with me.

But my bag is not in the Portuguese classroom.

And I don't even have Portuguese tutoring tomorrow.

I can't tell her any of that. I have to hide things just like she does.

"Well, I don't want you coming home all by yourself anymore," she says.

"I . . . I'll ask Leonor!" I say. Even though I just yelled at Leonor. Even though she'll probably never want to go back to that graveyard with me after I left her like that.

I need to find a way to get Leonor on my side.

I need some help to find the truth and I can't trust my mom to give it to me.

Mom thinks for a minute. Then nods.

"Alma, are you sure you're OK?" she asks again She puts her hands on my cheeks.

I can't tell her I'm not OK. I can't tell her Leonor says he's alive. And Leonor has no reason to lie. As much as I don't want to believe her, I'm starting to.

I can't mention in even the smallest, teeniest way that my dad is maybe possibly kind of alive because I know, know, know deep in my soul that if she finds out he *is* still alive, she will try to keep him from me.

Mom shuts my brain down. "Alma?"

"Yes!'" I say. "I'm fine! I'm just upset about my bag. I'm going to get so behind in my homework."

"Well," Mom says. "I guess maybe this will teach you to be more responsible for yourself."

Be responsible for myself. That's exactly what I have to do.

I have to be responsible for my own answers.

twenty
WHAT HAPPENED?

I LEAVE THE APARTMENT AS SOON as I'm dry. I tell Mom I'm going to ask Leonor about taking the trolley home with me tomorrow.

Really, I know I have to apologize to Leonor. I have to beg her to forgive me. Then, I have to figure out how to do the cousin-thing. How to be her friend. I have to find out everything she knows about my dad.

And I want to see avó. I want to search her face for the truth. If my dad is alive, she must know. I want to play music next to her and hope the notes seep information into my skull through some sort of family-magical bond.

Leonor opens the door. Avó isn't there.

Leonor stands in the doorway in fresh, dry clothes. Her dark blond hair is still wet and unwound from its braid, hanging in curly clumps around her face. I've never seen it down. It makes her look older. More intimidating.

"I guess it's my turn to say sorry." It takes me too long to say it.

She nods.

"I shouldn't have left you there. I just . . . I can't even . . ." I pause.

I study my cousin. She stands on the other side of the doorway, her arm stretched to hold the half door open for me.

"I don't know what to say except I'm sorry," I finish.

She nods again. "It must have been shocking. But I'm still your cousin," she says. "You shouldn't have left me there."

I chew my cheek, thinking. She seems to know the secret cousin code or something. Maybe she doesn't know she's my first cousin ever.

What can I do to make it up to her? To make her like me again?

I step inside. "Do you think you could braid my hair?" I ask.

Leonor clutches her hands to her chest just like avó does.

"Certainly!" she says. "We'll forget about this, this one time. As long as you promise it won't happen again."

"It won't," I say. "I promise." And I mean it. Leonor has to be on my team if I'm ever going to find my dad, dead or alive.

"Good," she says. "Because we're the cousins, you know? We're the . . . children . . . kids. We should be on the same team."

She turns to look at me and I nod and squint at her. She just said out loud what I'd been thinking. Maybe I do have a little bit of the secret cousin code.

It's easy to ask questions as she stands behind me braiding my hair. I don't even have to look at her face while she realizes how weird I am.

"So avó must have had a husband?" I say.

"Yes," Leonor says. "Vovô. Our funny vovô. He passed away a few years ago. He also played the piano. You would have liked him."

So they both play the piano. Both of my dad's parents. Does that mean my dad played? Plays?

"Was he my grandfather too? Like he was my dad's dad?" I ask.

I'm being so careful. It's the perfect way to bring up my dad without getting back into the argument.

"Of course," Leonor says. "Your dad's dad and my dad's dad. Our dads are full brothers." I tilt my head to the left and she uses her hand to straighten it. "Hold still," she says.

"Where is your dad?" I say, realizing I should have asked a long time ago. Maybe Leonor's dad is gone or in some sort of trouble. I should know by now why she lives with her grandmother instead of her parents.

"Oh, he's in the south of Portugal," Leonor says. "With the rest of the family. That's where we are all from. My parents send me and my siblings up here to go to the international school just so we can get a better education. So we've all taken turns living with avó. I'm the youngest."

"Oh," I say. "Do you miss him?"

Leonor pulls a chunk of hair over my right ear. "Of course," she says. "I can barely wait until mid-October when they will come for a visit. I usually go down to see them on the long weekends but this year they are coming up to see you."

"Yeah," I say. "My mom told me about that."

I try to brainstorm what to say next. How can I turn this into information I can use?

"Alma," Leonor says. "I know avó and your mother have told us not to discuss him but . . . can I ask you . . . What exactly is the story you know to be true about your father?"

She brought him up. Perfect!

"My mom told me he moved with her to America so that he could be there when I was born. And then he had a disease or something and he died when I was only a few weeks old."

Leonor tries to start the braid over. I can feel her fingers shaking as they comb through my hair.

"Oh," she says. Then nothing for a long time.

Finally she says, "I wonder where that story came from." She pauses. "He must have gone to Pennsylvania to meet you as a baby. And then come back here and disappeared. Maybe your mom assumed? Or maybe someone told her a falsehood?"

"What's the real story?" I ask. I know she doesn't have a reason to lie but how could he be alive this whole time? Where could he have been?

"I don't know it," Leonor says. "Not really."

"Oh," I say. "Why not?"

"Children are not supposed to have the details. At least

that's what my parents said. For a long time, all we only knew was that when I was very young, tio Jorge and avó had a big argument and then they didn't talk for a long time. Tio Jorge disappeared and no one knew where he was for years. Then he came back and was around every once in a while, then he disappeared again. Then he came back, and on and on. Right now no one knows where he is. My cousins and siblings and I have always wondered . . . It is the family mystery."

"I have to find out," I say.

I turn. I don't care if I mess up her braid. "You can't tell avó I'm looking for him, OK?" I say. "Not yet. I need to figure this out."

"We," Leonor says. "*We* can figure this out."

She starts to braid again. I sit quietly. I enjoy the pulling on my scalp. I focus on each strand of hair.

"Here you go," Leonor says. "I think it turned out quite nicely."

I can't see it of course, because it's on the back of my head.

"Let me run into avó's room and grab her mirror," Leonor says.

I nod. Then I'm alone in my grandmother's living room.

If Jorge is alive, why does my mom think he's dead?

The question runs in my brain over and over and over. I can't make it stop.

"Alma," Leonor calls from inside avó's room. "I had a thought. Would you like to see a picture?"

A picture!

I stand and sprint to the outside of avó's room.

"Come," Leonor says. "Before she gets home."

I walk over to the side of avó's bed. It's covered in a red duvet with brighter red flowers. The room smells like cinnamon. I feel sneaky walking into someone's room like this. Someone I barely know.

But she is my grandmother. My avó.

"Here," Leonor says, pointing up at a framed picture hanging next to the bed. It's large and it has a bunch of people in it, all posed like a professional family photo. I can tell by the clothes they are wearing that someone took this picture a long time ago.

"That's avó," she says, pointing. "And vovô. And their kids. So . . . our cousin Beatriz is in the picture. See?" She points to a baby. "Which means my dad would have been around twenty-eight so your dad would have been around twenty."

She points to a man sitting at his mom's feet.

She didn't need to point though.

I already knew it was him. His face is younger, but it's the same face. The same as the internet version I'd found back at home.

My dad is Internet Jorge Costa.

Internet Jorge Costa who is a landscaper or something in Lisbon.

Internet Jorge Costa who isn't married and has no kids.

Internet Jorge Costa who is alive.

My dad is alive.

And I already found him. I found him a long, long time ago.

I'm too stunned to react. Leonor just watches me stare at the picture.

He's smiling in it. Just like he does online.

There's the creak of the door in the other room and Leonor whispers, "Oh! Avó's home!"

We rush out the door and into the hallway.

"Hello, avó!" Leonor calls. "A Alma está aqui."

I know what that means. *Alma's here.*

"Estávamos só à procura de um espelho no teu quarto para que ela pudesse ver a trança que eu lhe fiz."

I panic for only a second. I hate being left out just because I don't speak the language. When it happens with family it's its own kind of loneliness. But right away Leonor turns to me and translates. "I just told her we were looking for the mirror so you could see your braid."

Leonor smiles at me. It's a kind of sly smile. The kind that's almost a wink.

I smile back at her.

I feel warmth in my blood when I look at her smile.

Right in this moment I like Leonor.

Avó clutches her hands to her chest at the sight of me. She pulls me into her arms and my head floats above hers. It's awkward but loving. She turns me around so she can see the braid. "Bonita!" she says.

"Beautiful," Leonor translates, even though I knew that one.

Avó keeps her hands tight on my shoulders. She turns to

Leonor and asks a question.

Then she pulls me close again.

Avó loves me. It's so clear that she loves me. She must have been waiting twelve years to hug me like this.

"She says would you like to stay for dinner?" Leonor says.

I nod. "Yes," I say. "Thank you. Obrigada."

Avó says a bunch more in Portuguese, then turns and pulls her cell phone out of her purse.

"She's texting your mom to make sure it's OK," Leonor says. "Then she wants to play piano with you while I make dinner."

I turn to her. I thought avó would make dinner.

"It's all right," Leonor says. "I don't mind. We're family."

A few minutes later my fingers are dancing on the piano keys next to my grandmother's. The sweet and salty aroma of Portuguese dinner mix behind my head. There is so much love in the room you can smell it.

My dad is alive.

He should be here.

I should have been here all along.

I have a family who acts like a family.

Maybe they only meant for my mom to believe he was dead.

Maybe I was supposed to be in on the secret from the start, only they couldn't get to me because my mom took me so far away from my people.

Maybe I never needed Mom and Adam anyway.

Maybe I was supposed to be on this side of the world all along.

That thought stays with me all through dinner and getting ready for bed. I settle into my bed barely saying good night to Mom. I am warm. I am happy. I am whole.

I am Portuguese.

I stay warm and comfortable like that until late into the night when I wake with a jolt, a question banging inside my head.

What happened?

If my dad didn't die . . . If he's still alive . . . where is he?

What happened?

twenty-one
WHAT IF?

LAST NIGHT. I FORGOT TO ASK Leonor if she would keep coming home from school with me on the trolley after my Portuguese tutoring, even though I ran away from her yesterday. Still, the minute I see her standing in her usual place waiting for me to walk to the trolley in the morning, I know she'll say sure.

Or she'll say something like "Certainly, I'd be honored."

She smiles at me as I approach and it's different. It's not a big and broad and overeager smile. Instead it's a small, knowing smile.

Leonor is still not someone I would have made friends with back at home. But maybe it's OK that I didn't have a choice here. Maybe it's good to have different sorts of friends that you wouldn't connect with unless you need to.

Maybe that's the entire point of cousins.

I ask Leonor if she'll escort me home. "It would be my pleasure," she says.

I smile to myself at her formality. I'm finding it a bit amusing. Maybe it's a little less annoying.

The truth is that I don't actually have to go to Portuguese tutoring after school today.

It takes me a minute to remember to tell Leonor that.

"Actually, I don't have Portuguese after school today. I just . . . I have to go back to the graveyard. To get my bag."

"Oh!" Leonor says. "I didn't realize you left it there." She looks worried.

I have to let her in. Just a little. If we're going to be the kind of close cousins she wants to be, I have to let her see how weird I am.

"It's OK," I say. "You don't have to come with me. I don't mind being in graveyards by myself."

"You don't?" she asks, surprised. "You don't find them creepy?"

"No," I say. "I actually like them. I went to graveyards all the time back home. But don't tell my mom that."

Leonor smiles. If she thinks I'm weird she doesn't let me know. "OK, then," she says. "You run to the graveyard after school to see if your bag is there. I will wait for you in the school yard."

"Perfect," I say.

When we sit on the trolley, Leonor leans into me to

whisper in my ear. "I plan to call my mother as soon as we arrive home today. My father is consistently . . . what do you say? Tight-lipped. But I can sometimes get a fact or two out of my mother."

My eyes go wide. "Thank you!" I say.

She nods. "I am going to help you. We are going to find him. Whatever it is that happened, he is your father and you need to meet him."

The school day ticks by slowly. The lessons and lunch and recreation go on around my head. Inside all I can think about is my dad.

It's like the first day of school all over again. Except now, my dad is alive.

At the end of the day I slip out the front doors to the school in the wave of my classmates. Leonor said she'd wait for me in the school yard so I'll go find her there in an hour or so. First I sneak through the woods and follow along the concrete wall until I'm at the entrance to the graveyard again.

I take a deep breath and my heart calms down. There's still a pulling on the middle chamber. I walk to where I left Leonor yesterday and there's my bag in a wet heap on the grass. I pick it up and there are goose bumps running up and down my spine despite the sun shining above me.

I must be crazy. He's alive. I know he's alive now. But I still feel him in this graveyard.

*   *   *

When I get home, I open my tablet to Skype Julia. I've known my dad is alive for twenty-four hours and I still haven't told her yet.

I also haven't talked to her in days.

I miss her desperately.

But when my finger hovers over the Skype button, it starts shaking.

What will Julia say if she finds out he's alive? Will she be mad about all the time I made her spend in graveyards this summer?

Will she say terrible things about my mom because she didn't look hard enough for the truth?

Will she say I'm not safe with my Portuguese family because somewhere in the midst of it there's someone who lied?

Or will she say something worse . . . something about my dad and why everyone told me he was dead?

I can't do it.

I can't let her ruin him before I've found him.

In my heart he's perfect. I can't share him with anyone who might not see him that way.

I open up my email and send her a short note instead, about Portuguese tutoring and today's school lunch and playing piano with my grandmother. I leave out the parts I'd usually want to tell. I give her a nice, normal email like I'm the nice, normal best friend she deserves.

Then I go downstairs.

Leonor answers the door again. She pulls me inside, then locks it behind me like we are spies trading top secret information.

A little rush of happiness goes through my blood. Looking for my dad is fun with Leonor in a way it was never fun with Julia. The thought makes me feel guilty.

Leonor pulls me into her bedroom and sits me down on her bed. "I'm afraid I don't have any more information as far as where or how to find him," she says. My heart falls. "My mother either does not know or is refusing to give me that information."

"OK," I say. My brain starts to spin. There has to be another way.

"However," Leonor says, "I did acquire one small idea as to why tio Jorge disappeared from the family in the first place. And why avó can't seem to forgive him even though she keeps trying."

I look up at my cousin who is standing above me, twin braids framing the sides of her face. "Yeah?" I say.

"The first fight," she says. "The one that caused a rift in the family that has still not mended . . . she told me what it was about."

"And?" I say.

Leonor swallows. "You," she says. "The fight was about you."

"Me?" I say.

Leonor nods. "Tio Jorge lost you. That's what my mom said. By the time avó knew of your existence, he had lost you to America. And avó has missed you ever since."

He lost me.

Part of my brain tells me it couldn't be that simple, but the sentence makes me feel good. He lost me. That's all. If he only lost me, he can find me again. He can Google my name and he'll see my picture in the paper from my piano recital last year. Or he can Google Mom's name and he'll see her contact information for her business. Or he can . . .

I look up at Leonor.

"Oh my gosh!" I say. "*I* have a clue."

"You do?" she says, shocked.

"Do you have a computer?" I ask.

She nods.

"I found a page on him," I say. "I Googled. I found him on social media."

"Really? Truly?" Leonor says.

"Yes!" I say. "Really and truly."

"My family has tried this . . . He must have blocked—"

I don't want to hear that. I interrupt her. "Let's go get my tablet then," I say.

We rush upstairs and into my bedroom. I pull up his page in less than a minute. "But it's all in Portuguese," I say.

Leonor smiles a sneaky half smile. "Well, I know Portuguese," she says. "Let's email him now."

"Email him?" I ask. "How?

Leonor points to the side of the screen, some more words

in Portuguese. "That says 'send a private message.'"

My eyes go wide. But then I nod.

That night I barely sleep.

Instead, over and over again, I picture Internet Jorge Costa opening his PMs and staring at Leonor's words. I don't even know what exactly she said. In the end I was too scared to be in the same room with her as she wrote the email.

The email to my dad.

My dad who is supposed to be dead.

What if he doesn't want to see me?

What if he doesn't check his messages?

What if? What if? What if?

The questions are running through my head the whole next morning. Mom keeps asking me what's wrong. "You look like you've seen a ghost," she says.

I haven't, not yet. But I'm trying to.

"I'm just tired," I tell her, and rush off to meet Leonor at the trolley stop.

"Cousin!" she says as she sees me walking though the crowded, narrow streets of Lisbon.

"Hi," I say, walking up beside her.

She won't know anything yet. I remind myself. *She only emailed him last night.*

She leans close to me and whispers, "Do you have tutoring after school today?"

I shake my head no.

"Did you tell your mom one way or the other?"

"No," I say.

My hands start to shake. What is she getting at?

"Well, good," she says. "Then you're going to meet him."

"What!" My jaw drops. "Today?"

Leonor nods. "Today. He wrote back right away. He will meet you after school."

I take a deep breath. My shoulders relax. Of course he did. Of course he wrote back as soon as he found out I was here.

He's my dad after all.

He's my *dad.*

"Where?" I say.

Leonor smiles. "I wasn't sure where to suggest. He says he has a job landscaping somewhat near to our school. And since we are only children, we are limited as to where we can go."

I nod.

"So, I suggested, perhaps . . . Well, I hope this idea sits well with you. I suggested he meet you in the cemetery? The one you were searching for him in the first place."

I smile. "Cousin," I say for the first time. "That's perfect."

The school day passes in a blur of nervous excitement. I've arranged to meet Leonor in the school library at four thirty. She offered to come with me, but she also said my dad speaks English. I decided to go on my own. I decided I didn't want any filter, anything getting in the way of seeing exactly how much he loves me.

When the school day is finally over, I walk slowly and carefully to the graveyard. Part of me wants to run there, but I don't want to show up sweaty and out of control. I want to look put together. I don't want him to see how desperately I've missed him.

Not first. Not until I see how desperately he's missed me.

My heart is pounding so hard I can see it shaking my uniform shirt. My palms are sweaty as I walk through the gate to the graveyard.

I have to remind myself not to read the headstones. He is here, but he's above the ground.

I walk down the main street toward the grave-mansion. I don't see anyone, so I walk around to the back.

There is a man bent over behind a tree. Big scary boots. My heart somehow finds a way to pound harder.

"Excuse me?" I say.

The man straightens up. He's not so tall and he's too young and his hair isn't gray at all. It's not him. "Não falo inglês," he says. "No English."

"Oh," I say.

I think for a minute.

This is not what I've been picturing all day. This is not what I thought it would be like when I imagined returning here to actually find my father.

Then I realize I do know what to say.

"Jorge Costa?"

The young man's eyes light up with recognition. "Jorge?" he says. "Um minuto."

He takes off in a little golf cart and I stand there and press my hands together.

I don't know what I'm going to say.

I don't know what I'm going to do.

I don't even know how to feel.

I wait and wait until I hear the little golf cart coming from behind me. I don't turn. I got all the way to Portugal. I searched for him for years. I'm going to make him cross the last distance.

"Alma," he says, walking around to face me.

I finally turn and look at him.

I see avó Flávia in the shape of his eyes. I see the same dark eyes and wrinkles in his forehead that were on his father in the picture in avó's room.

He smiles.

In his smile, I see my own.

My pounding heart slows just a little bit. My fingers relax at my sides. This is my dad. This is finally my dad.

This is the moment I've thought about forever. This is the moment that was never supposed to happen.

"You're here," Jorge says. "Does your mom know you're here?"

I shake my head no.

Jorge nods. "Not at all?" he says.

"I mean, she knows I'm in Portugal, in Lisbon, of course,

because she's here too. We're living above avó's apartment. But . . . she thinks I'm at school."

He nods again. "OK," he says.

"My school is right over there," I say. "So it's not like a big lie or anything."

I've known my dad for less than five minutes and I'm already more honest with him than I am with my mom.

"OK," he says again.

I'm somehow surprised by how thick his accent is. It's even thicker than Leonor's. I can't hear myself in his voice at all.

"Come on," he says. He walks back toward the golf cart. "Let's talk."

I take a beat before I follow him.

Can I follow him?

Could he be dangerous?

"Wait," I say. He turns. "Are you really him?"

He studies my face like he isn't sure what to answer. Or whether to answer.

"Are you really my dad?"

He nods.

I follow him.

We drive the golf cart slowly through the winding alleys of the graveyard and out through a back entrance I've never seen before. We drive a few blocks and then he pulls into a drive-way next to a Portuguese mansion. "Turns out I'm working over here these days," he says. "Right by your school."

I nod.

"So this was easy. After all this time. Who would have thought?"

"Yeah," I say. I try to say something else. I'm too overwhelmed. I don't know where to begin.

I know I need to ask questions. This is the parent who I've always known would tell me everything. But I don't want to say the wrong thing. The thing that would make him disappear again.

Of course, if this is my honest parent, my never-lying-never-sneaky parent, why does my mom think he's dead?

I put my hands in front of my face, trying to physically shove that thought out of my brain. Jorge doesn't seem to notice.

"Come in," he says, getting out of the cart and walking around the back to a small shed next to the mansion.

I follow him. I'm nervous until I see the inside. There are lockers around the walls and a TV much too big for the wall it's on. There are folding chairs scattered about the floor. A big window across from the TV lets in plenty of light.

"The boss for this job is all right," Jorge says, pointing out the door toward the mansion behind us. "They let us have this little area to take some breaks."

Jorge flips on the TV. The screen turns green, and black stick-figure soccer players bounce in the middle of it.

"*Sonic Soccer*," Jorge says, even though I already know the game. "You know how to play?"

I nod. I push the image out of my head. I pretend I don't see Adam's hands on the controller next to mine as he refuses to let me win.

How can I still miss Adam?

How can I want another dad when I've finally found the right one? When he's alive? When he's right here?

"Let's play," he says.

I should ask him what happened. I should ask him why he never tried to find me. Why I had to find him.

Why my mom thinks he's dead.

But I just sit in the folding chair next to him and we begin the game. I score a goal in the first minute.

"Wow!" he says.

But I can tell he let me score.

"How do you know how to play?" he asks.

"My stepfather," I say. "He taught me."

Jorge nods. "He's here with you now?" he says. "In Portugal?"

"No," I say. I wait a minute before I say, "They got divorced."

I'm doing what he told me to do though. Adam. I'm being honest with the people who love me.

Because Jorge must love me, right? Or he will love me? He's my dad.

We play for a minute. Then another. Another. Too many minutes go by without any words. This is not OK. This is not what I was picturing. I thought my dad would be full of chatter and stupid jokes. I thought he'd cook for me and drive me places and show up to cheer for me at piano recitals.

I never once pictured him playing video games.

Time ticks by. I look at the clock on the wall and realize I have to get back to school in twenty minutes.

"So," I say. "Why . . . why now?" I think about how to go on. How to ask more without scaring him. "What . . . Where did you think I was? And why . . . why don't I know you?"

Jorge coughs so loudly I stop talking.

"Alma," Jorge says. He says it like avó does. He says it in Portuguese.

I should have been hearing my name said like that my entire life.

"We're here now. Together. Let's enjoy it."

"But," I say. "But why—"

He cuts me off again. "Who wants the unpleasant details when we could just enjoy each other's company?"

I do. I want the unpleasant details. And the pleasant ones. I want all the details.

"I . . . I want to know . . . I need—"

"Listen," Jorge says. "I will tell you. I'll make sure you understand. But let me . . . let me get to know you first. It's too . . . soon. Too difficult too soon. Give me a few days."

My heart squeezes and contracts. I can't fit it into the tiny place it wants to go.

"No!" I want to say. "No! No! No! You are supposed to be the parent who gives me answers. You are supposed to be the parent who sees me as a full person who deserves her full story. You are supposed to tell me what happened."

But I'm sure that would be the wrong thing to say.

The thing that would make him disappear all over again.

I focus on the *give me a few days*. I'll see him again. In just a few days.

I score on him. Then I say, "It's hard to enjoy your company when you're letting me win."

He laughs a big, bright, open laugh that is so unlike my mom it makes my heart grow a little closer to its normal size. "OK, then," he says.

With two flicks of his thumbs his players are behind me and he scores.

"What do you say again?" he says. "Game on!"

I stand up to make my players charge back at him. "Take that!" I say.

He laughs again. I make him laugh.

I make my dad laugh.

Twenty minutes later, Jorge drives the golf cart to the edge of the woods to drop me off close to school.

"Come see me again?" he says.

His eyes are shining. The smile on his face matches the smile on mine.

"Yes," I say. "I can't see you tomorrow though. I have Portuguese tutoring after school."

He'll ask me a question now. All day I've been waiting for him to ask me a question. It'll be a simple one like *Oh, you don't speak any Portuguese?* or *Oh, you're trying to learn the language?*

He doesn't.

"The day after, then," he says. "You can meet me at my shed. Just knock on the door."

I nod.

"Oh!" he says. "I almost forgot. I got you something."

He reaches into the little compartment in the golf cart that's between our seats. He pulls out a small white box tied up with red-and-white string and hands it to me.

I pull the string to untie it. I open the box.

"Pastel de nata," he says. "My favorite Portuguese treat."

I pinch my lips together and bite down with my teeth to keep myself from saying "I knew it! I knew it! When I ate one of these the first time I knew you must love them as much as I do."

"Thank you," I say finally.

"Do you want to try it?" he asks.

I stare at it. It's sitting perfectly in the center of the little square box. Its crust is crinkled symmetrically. The waning sunlight reflects off the burnt-sugar top.

"I will later," I say. "When I'm good and hungry."

He chuckles.

But I know I won't. I just told a lie. That is the first lie I've ever told my dad.

I'll never eat this pastel de nata. I'll put it on my window-sill next to the fresh flowers. I'll keep it there as it melts and grows moldy and even if it stinks. I'll never get rid of this. The first thing my father gave me.

Proof that he could have loved me all along.

He chuckles again. "Well, just don't tell your mom where you got it from."

I push those words out of my head as I climb out of the golf cart and watch him disappear back in the direction of the mansion and the shed.

I think instead about my treat.

About my dad.

About how my dad gave me something. My dad did something just for me.

That night I don't Skype Julia.

I don't go downstairs and talk to Leonor.

I avoid my mom.

I sit by the window in my bedroom and stare at my pastel de nata.

Leonor and Julia would ask me all the questions he didn't answer. They'd make me feel like today was less than perfect because there are so many questions still in the air.

If my mom finds out he's alive, she'll be afraid of me finding answers and then I'll never find them.

No one could understand what happened to me today.

None of them could understand how a little pastry could mean so much in the face of all these mysteries.

twenty-two
WHAT IS A DAD?

I GO SEE JORGE AGAIN TWO days later after school. Leonor has been asking about the first time over the past few days but I tell her a need a little time to figure out how to talk about it. I tell her I've been missing my dad for twelve years and I need to spend some more time with him before I start to talk about it. She seems to understand, but she keeps asking anyway.

I have to get some answers today so that I can tell her something.

I walk up to the shed outside the mansion and knock.

"Alma," Jorge says, opening the door and standing aside so I can walk in. I immediately see a guitar leaning against the chair. He notices me notice it. "She's beautiful, right?" he says about the guitar. He holds it

I take the guitar from him like he indicates. I sit and strum an easy A, B-flat, A.

"You already know," he says, smiling.

"A little," I say. "I'm better at piano."

"I can't stand the piano," he says.

I pretend it doesn't sting.

"So why has it been so long?" I say. I'm not waiting to ask my questions. I need answers. I know that Mom won't give them to me and Adam won't and Flávia can't. And Leonor barely knows more than me. This is the adult who I've always known would give me the answers.

"What you mean so long?" he says. "So long since I last played guitar?" He takes the guitar back from me and sits across from me.

I lower my eyebrows at him. I have no idea when he last played guitar. I know almost nothing about him. That's the problem.

"No. So long without us seeing each other," I say, choosing the words carefully.

"We saw each other two days ago," he says. He starts strumming a song I don't recognize.

This is starting to feel like talking to my mom. But no. It can't. It can't be like that.

"I mean before that. You hadn't seen me since I was a baby."

Jorge stops playing and looks right at my face. "Since you were a baby?" he says.

"Yeah," I say. "I mean . . . what happened?"

He sighs and plays another chord.

"What else has your mother told you?" he asks.

My fingers start to wiggle at my sides. I wish I had a guitar or something to keep my hands and eyes busy. I don't think I can tell the truth on this one. "Nothing," I say. "She doesn't tell me anything."

I don't say "she thinks you're dead."

I don't want to start giving him answers until I have mine.

"What did she say when you told her you'd found me?" he asks carefully.

I can't answer that either. He's a stranger but he's also my dad. I have no idea what is safe to tell him. It's so confusing.

"I have questions!" I blurt, exasperated. "I always thought that if I could find you, you'd give me answers."

His face softens. "You always thought that, huh?" he says. He pats the folding chair next to him, indicating that I should sit in it.

I do.

"Yeah," I say.

He takes a deep breath. "You know, Alma," he says. "Everyone has their own stories. I can't give you answers about your mother or anything else."

"I know," I say. My heart is calming down. He's not sidestepping. He's talking to me directly.

"You trusted me before you met me, huh?" he says.

I think about that for a minute. "I guess I did," I say.

He nods. "Then maybe you can trust me now. I'll tell you my story. It just . . . it just might take a little while. OK? I need to get to know you. I need you to get to know me. We need to spend some time together before any of the past can make any sort of sense."

Part of me wants to just say OK. He's my dad and I've missed him for so long and I want to make him happy.

"When do you think you can tell me?"

But instead of answering, he plays louder. "This is my favorite American song," he says. Then he plays the cords. D, E7, G, A. I know what it is right away. *Well she was an American girl.*

After a bar he hands the guitar back to me. I continue where he left off. D, E7, G, A. *She couldn't help thinking that there was a little more to life, somewhere else.*

My fake Portuguese lesson goes like this. The guitar going back and forth. The words all singing and no answers.

I don't ask what I need to. I let the questions haunt me. I bathe in the music.

I go back again a few days later, and again after the next weekend. Every time I don't have Portuguese tutoring after school, I pretend I do so that I can go see my dad.

He doesn't do any of the things I always thought he would. He doesn't give me anything else after the pastel de nata. He doesn't cook. He doesn't make silly jokes. He doesn't ask about school or my mom or my friends or my life. Either of my lives.

He tells me one thing that lets me know he's my dad though. He tells me he loves the graveyard.

He wasn't dead, but he loves a graveyard.

That explains why I always felt him there.

Even if the him I felt seemed like he'd be different than who he's really turning out to be.

He shows me around the graveyard. He tells me it's called the *Cemitério dos Prazeres,* the Cemetery of Pleasures. Apparently it's called that because this part of Lisbon is called *Prazeres.* But I also think it's the right name for this place. It's full of plants and colorful doors and every cheerful thing missing from other cemeteries.

I try to tell him that, but Jorge doesn't ask why I've spent so much time in so many other cemeteries.

Jorge doesn't ask any questions and he doesn't answer any either.

Every time I start to say the word *why* he says, "Alma, I will tell you everything soon."

When I keep asking he changes his answer to "Sometimes it seems like you're just here for the details instead of to get to know your own father." And I don't want him to feel that way, so I stop asking.

I trust him. I force myself to trust him. To believe he'll answer me soon.

Some days we play video games. Some days we play guitar. Some days we wander the graveyard and he complains about his boss, who makes him work extra hard even though he doesn't ever seem to really be working. He shows me trees he's planted and gardens he's arranged on his boss's property.

But he doesn't seem humble or brave or funny, like the dad

I pictured back in the old cemetery behind my old house. He's nothing like what I pictured. At least not yet.

One night in early October, a few weeks after I first met Jorge, I'm up late tossing and turning. I've been trying to get used to my new life, my new school, my new cousin, my new secret I keep from my mom. It all swirls and gets stuck in my brain when it's time for me to go to sleep.

A tiny sound coming from my top night table drawer rescues me from my own thoughts. It's my tablet.

It's Julia.

I listen to be sure I can hear my mom snoring through the wall, then I yank it out and open it.

"Alma!" she says. "I thought you forgot all about me!"

I should have called Julia weeks ago when I first found him. I should have told her right away.

But I can't say anything.

I can't tell her I finally found my dad but all he does is play video games and the guitar and complain about work.

I can't tell her he doesn't cook like her dad. He doesn't joke like her dad. He doesn't answer my questions or even ask me any.

I can't tell her that the person we searched for, the person we thought was lovely and then died, isn't dead and isn't alive. He never existed in the first place.

"I'm sorry," I say. "I've been so busy and the time change."

"I know, I know," Julia says. "I'm just glad you didn't make a new best friend in that new cousin you found and forget all about me."

My face burns. I don't tell Julia that Leonor sort of is my new best friend. That I go to her apartment after dinner most days and let her braid my hair. That she knows Jorge is alive. That she knows I'm keeping secrets and she may not know what they are, but she knows, at least, that there are secrets to be kept. That it feels good to share this mystery with her because Jorge was—is—her uncle. He belongs to her too, in a way he can never belong to Julia.

"Of course not," I say.

I don't know what else to say.

"How's school?"

I sound like an old person.

"Never mind that," Julia says. "Did you find him?"

I smile at her. Maybe I can give her just a tiny bit of the truth.

"Yes!" I say. "But you can't tell anyone."

"Was he in the graveyard?"

I think for just a second. It's true that technically I found him online, but the first time I saw him was in the graveyard. I decide to tell the truth in a way she will think is just me being my usual weird self.

"Really, he found me in the graveyard."

"He was in the graveyard? For real?" Julia says. "Right by your school?"

"He was!" I say.

She looks so happy for me. I beam back at her.

"Tell me about it," she says.

I take a deep breath. I think about all the graveyards I searched with Julia so long ago. I think about all the headstones she read with me. I think about the JFC headstone behind my old house and how sure I was about so many things.

I pretend my dad is that one. The one who was dead. The one who loved me so much and would have told me everything.

"It's small," I tell her. "The graveyard is full of these big headstones, the size of small houses. They all have flowers and etched windows and all these fancy things. But not my dad's. His is small. It just says his name. He must have been so humble."

"Wow," Julia says. "That's just like the headstone you thought was his all along."

My eyes burn. How can I be missing a headstone? I have an actual dad, but I'm missing a fake headstone.

"I know," I say.

We talk for a few more minutes, until I'm yawning so much that Julia says we should try to talk tomorrow.

I want to talk to her again tomorrow, of course.

But eventually it's going to be hard to keep up with all these lies.

* * *

Today is the day, I tell myself the next afternoon. I'm done keeping secrets from Leonor. I hate lying to Julia. I hate being the sneaky one between my mom and me. Today I get answers.

I'm walking to the shed, yawning after being up so late talking to Julia.

Today I find Jorge planting a flowering bush with a few other guys. I watch him for a minute, which I always do, until he comes to a point where he can take a break in his work.

"Alma," he says. "Let's take a walk."

My heart speeds up. A walk. He's never said that to me before. Usually when grown-ups say "walk" they really mean "talk."

Maybe my answers are coming without me even asking the questions.

We wind though the Portuguese-suburb streets to the front of the graveyard, then down the main path. It's a beautiful day with a blue sky and the sun beating down on my head. There are a few other people—mourners or tourists—wandering between the pristine white stone grave-houses. I wonder if they notice me walking next to Jorge. I wonder if we look like father and daughter. If we look normal.

"I have to tell you something," he says.

I hold my breath. This is it.

"I'm not going to be here tomorrow," he says.

I let my breath out. "OK," I say. "I'll just come back next week then."

He shakes his head. He bends over to straighten a flower that was leaning out of its flowerpot in front of Gloria Lopes's grave-house. But I think he just doesn't want to look at me.

"That's not what I mean," he says. "This job is over. The yard is all landscaped. I'm moving on."

"What?" I say, too loud for the graveyard. "Where are you going?"

He shrugs. "It's about an hour away in a town called Mafra."

"But—but—but—" I stammer.

"I can't help it, you know," he says. "I have to go where my job sends me."

"But how will I see you?" I manage.

"You still want to see me?" he asks, his eyes not leaving the flowerpot.

Words rush to my mouth.

Yes!

Of course!

Don't you still want to see me?

You promised to give me answers!

I won't let any of them out. I won't let myself cry.

He turns to look at me. "Alma," he says, "this is really all I have to offer. Video games and a little guitar."

"What about your story?" I ask. "You promised me some answers. You said to trust you."

He shrugs. "I guess I can't . . . I don't know . . . There's only so much I can give. Hasn't this month been enough?"

This month? He's been gone for all twelve years of my life

and he thinks a month of guitar and video games should be enough?

I can't cry.

I can't cry in front of this man.

This man is *not* my dad. My dad was full of questions and answers. My dad was cooking food for me and kissing my forehead before I fell asleep at night. My dad was holding hands with my mom in a way I would have to pretend to be embarrassed about. My dad was the loudest voice at my soccer games and piano recitals. I knew him so well when I thought he was underground.

"I don't know what you want from me," he says. "Mercy said she was bringing you here, that you needed to get to know me . . . I was happy to be able to meet you without her involved. But you know me now. That's really it."

"My mom didn't say that," I say. I'm being too loud. Way too loud. The tourists will stop and stare.

"Shh," Jorge says. "Yes, she did."

"My mom thinks you're dead," I spit.

"What?" he says. "Since when?"

"I don't know," I say. "But she does. My entire life she told me you were dead. Why do you think I was looking for you in a graveyard?"

"Alma," Jorge says, like I'm being ridiculous. He takes a step toward me and I flinch. I suddenly don't want him anywhere near me. He doesn't touch me and that's when I realize he never has. Not one hug. Not a pat on the head. Not even a handshake.

He pulls something out of his back pocket and hands it to me.

An envelope. "Here, open this."

It's a picture of me. My fifth grade school picture. There's a note written in Portuguese but I'd recognize the handwriting anywhere. It's Mom's.

"She's been writing to me your entire life," Jorge says. He's wearing a goofy smile like he just proved me wrong about some silly childhood misconception. Like this is a small detail. Like this is nothing. "I don't think she thinks I'm dead."

I stare at his face, his stupid smile, for just a second. My heart aches like someone punched it. I miss my fake dad. I miss Internet Jorge Costa so much. I can never look at that smile and feel warm and comfortable again.

Then I turn and run.

twenty-three
WHO ELSE HAS BEEN LYING?

WHEN I GET HOME, MY MOM is in the shower. It feels like the first good thing that's happened to me in weeks.

I throw down my backpack and sneak into her room and take her phone.

There's someone I need to confront even more than my mom.

I almost call but then I think better of it. I text him. I write "It's Alma. Call me" then I delete the text. That way it'll look like he called to check up on me again instead of like I called him.

He calls almost immediately.

I don't even say hello. I say, "I found him."

It's a trap and he walks right in.

"Your father?" Adam says. "She finally told you?"

My face flushes red-hot. I didn't know I could get any more angry today but now I am. I guess somewhere deep inside me I was hoping Adam didn't know. I was hoping there was still one person I could trust.

"You knew!" I yelp. "I knew you knew!"

"Alma," he says. "Calm down. It's OK."

"No it's not!" I say. "Nothing is OK. Nothing. You knew and you didn't tell me. I always knew my mother was a liar, but you!"

"What did she tell you?" he says, hushed.

I sit down on the bed. I feel a disgusting sort of power. I am so right about this. I am so angry about this. It makes me care about nothing else. It makes me able to demand exactly what I want. Need.

"Nothing," I say. "You think she'd actually tell me something?"

"What do you mean?" Adam says.

"She never tells me anything. She only lies," I say.

"Calm down, Alma-bear," he says. "Start at the beginning. Tell me exactly what happened. Everything."

"He met me in this graveyard," I say. "This gorgeous grave-yard with little houses instead of headstones."

I pause. I really did love that graveyard. I loved all the graveyards when the dad I was picturing was never there. Was never anywhere. Did I love graveyards because he did? This man who is basically a stranger? Do I still love them? Will I still hang out in graveyards? Will I even notice them anymore?

My whole life has been about the death of someone who is alive.

What am I going to do with myself now?

"Oh, Alma. You were in a graveyard?" Adam says. "I don't think you found him, sweetheart. Remember he has a very common name."

"I don't mean I saw his headstone. He met me there. Alive!"

"Oh," Adam says.

"My cousin helped me find him. He's a landscaper and he was working near my school. It's so . . . weird," I cry. "I knew his picture from the internet. Or I knew *a* picture from the internet. I never thought it could be him. You always said that thing about a common name—"

"Well, when I said that—" Adam tries, but it's my turn. I keep talking.

"But it turns out all these years I was staring at the right picture! Then Leonor emailed him and . . . we found him . . . So then she suggested we meet in this graveyard. And then we did."

"Alma, are you sure—"

"And I asked him 'Are you my dad?' and he said yes. And then we played *Sonic Soccer* in Portuguese."

"Whoa," Adam says. "Wait a minute."

But I don't. I'm done listening to grown-ups who don't tell me the truth.

"And he showed me some guitar chords. And he showed me around the graveyard. And we played more video games. And then today he shows me this picture of me from just last year with a note from Mom. Do you know what that means, Adam? Do you?"

"Honey, does your mom know about all of this?"

"It means she *knew* he was alive. All the time she knew he was alive and she *kept* him from me."

It occurs to me that maybe she kept him from me because he wasn't the humble and brave chef, comedian, soccer-and-piano superfan I always imagined him to be.

But still. I should have known that. I should have known that the whole time.

"Why did everyone say he was dead?"

"Alma . . ." Adam says. Then stops.

"You have to tell me," I say. "Everything you know. You have to tell me now."

Anger is making me powerful. I can make him tell me the truth. I can force it.

"Sweetheart, I can't. Mercy has to—"

"This is why you couldn't adopt me," I say. "Isn't it?"

"Alma," he says as if it's an answer. Alma has only ever been a question.

"No!" I say. "Tell me. This is why, right? Because I had some dad I wasn't allowed to know anything about? That meant I couldn't have another dad who actually loved me?"

"It's so complicated, sweetheart."

"Answer me!" I say. "That's why, isn't it?"

"Well, technically, yes, but—"

"Why didn't you tell me?" I say. I can feel the power

slipping away. Tears are close by. I'm nauseous now.

"I didn't know," Adam says. We're talking so fast. It's like he knows Mom is going to be out of the shower soon. It's like he knows we only have a little time. But really I think he's matching my pace. "I didn't know when I asked that, when I asked about . . . about adopting you. She didn't tell me until after I asked. I didn't know he was alive either. Not until she had to tell me I couldn't adopt you without his permission."

"You should have told me!" I say.

"I didn't know!" Adam says again.

"No!" I say. "Once you knew! Once you knew you should have told me," I say.

"I couldn't!" Adam says. "It wasn't my place."

I don't have time to argue that. I have to get to the truth.

"Tell me now," I say. "Tell me everything you know."

"Alma," he says. "Mercy has to—"

"No!" I cry again. "My dad is alive. He's alive. And she knew it. Do you think I can ever believe anything she says ever again? I need you to tell me everything."

"I'm sorry," he says. "I'm so sorry, sweetheart."

"You wanted to adopt me. You wanted to be my dad which would make you just as able to tell me as my mom."

"What can I do, Alma? I'll do anything. But your mom has to—"

"You said you loved me! You said you loved me more than yourself! You said you loved me like your own!"

"I did," he says. "I do. I would have adopted you in a heartbeat. I do love you."

I'm crying now. I'm crying so hard I can't yell anymore. I think he's crying too.

"Adam," I say. "I can't."

"Alma, sweetheart," he says. "I know this is hard. It's going to be the hardest thing you've ever been through. But your mother will tell you everything. You go tell her what you told me and she'll tell you everything now. I can feel it. She'll finally let it go."

"I can't, Adam," I say. "I don't think I can."

"You have to, sweetheart. You're keeping secrets just like her. You're telling lies to keep those secrets. If you don't break this habit, you'll be doing that your entire life. It's been so hard on your mother, such a weight for her to carry. And of course it's awful for you too. You go be the honest one. You can fix the whole family."

"I can't, Adam. I can't . . . anything."

"You can't what?" he says.

"Something needs to happen," I say. "Something I can know."

"Alma, baby," he says. "What do you mean?"

"When you told me all that," I say. "When you told me you loved me like that. Like you didn't know you could. Like your own . . ."

"Yes," Adam says. "I meant every word."

"I believed you then but I . . . I can't. I can't. I don't anymore. I don't think I can believe anything."

"Alma, my Alma. I love you. I do love you. You have to
believe me."

And I try. I try hard to search my heart for some sign of
love coming in. From Adam. Or my mom. Or avó. Or Leonor.
Or Julia. But my heart isn't working. It closed up shop. Nothing coming in, nothing going out.

Nothing.

twenty-four
HOW DO I STOP BEING A SNEAKY KID?

LEONOR BECOMES THE FIRST PERSON IN my new truthful life. She helped me find Jorge and I should have been telling her all along how he was disappointing me. I shouldn't have been so sneaky. It feels weird to tell the truth. After school, we walk through the Cemetery of Pleasures even though I know he won't be there. His name won't be on the headstones and he won't be wandering around admiring the landscaping. I need to see it for myself. To see the place empty. To know that he's gone and that he really thought guitar chords and video games and the one stupid pastel de nata were enough.

"I'm sorry I wouldn't tell you anything," I say when I finish the story. "I kept hoping he would change. He would magically start giving me answers. He would . . . be the dad I always wanted. I was afraid you'd point out all the ways he was disappointing me before I was ready to admit it. But he's not. He's not the dad I always wanted. I should have told you everything the whole time. You could have helped. I know that now. I'm sorry. Desculpa."

"See?" Leonor says, smiling. "You have been learning some Portuguese anyway."

I wonder if she can really forgive me this quickly.

I look at her and try to open my heart. If she forgives me that quickly, she must love me. I try to let some of the love in. But I can't. My heart is shut down for business.

We keep walking through the graveyard. She stops to study a grave. One of the smaller ones that looks like it can't be much bigger than a closet inside. Still, it has an etched glass over the stones where the windows should be. It has a little porch with a pointed roof. It's small but it's still too fancy for my dead dad who never existed anywhere except inside my head.

"This place really is quite beautiful," Leonor says. "I never thought to spend time in graveyards."

"I know," I say. "I'm weird."

I feel calm in this graveyard. Even though I'm so sad I didn't know sadness this deep existed before, I still feel calm here. Maybe I always will.

"We have to get to the bottom of it," Leonor says. She pulls her jacket tighter around her uniform. There is a chill in the air although I didn't notice it until I saw her do that. The sky above us is darkening already. We're inching into the rainy season as Leonor calls winter. Back in Pittsburgh, it's almost fall break.

"Get to the bottom of what?" I ask.

"What happened," she says. "To your dad."

"But nothing happened to him. I just told you. He's still here. He's a landscaper. He never left Lisbon."

"Yeah," Leonor says. "But why? Why did your mom tell you he was dead?"

To keep him from me.

"Why did he have that big fight with avó? Why do they have such a hard time getting along? Why doesn't he ever come to family gatherings, like the one we're having this weekend?"

I freeze. I had forgotten all about the cousins and aunts and uncles all coming to Lisbon to meet me. "That's this weekend?" I ask. I shiver. "Do you think he'll be there?"

Leonor shakes her head. "He's invited of course, but he never comes. We've only seen him every few years since you were born, and it's gone badly each time. Then years go by before avó begs him to come around and then when he does they fight again."

"Why?" I ask. I do sort of want to know. How did I cause a fight between avó and Jorge? And how did that end up meaning I thought he was dead for all these years?

"Let's try to figure something out," Leonor says. "When did your mother first say he died?"

"The story was that he died right when I was born," I say.

"No," Leonor says. "I mean when did she *tell* you? How old were you? Where were you?"

I close my eyes and let my brain rewind through the entire History of Questions. I'm remembering so many *I'll tell you when your older*s and *Please don't ask me that*s. My brain gets stuck on a loop until it finally reaches through to the beginning.

"Wait a minute," I say. "She didn't . . . She didn't tell me he was dead."

"She didn't?" Leonor says.

"No . . . it wasn't her."

"Then who did?"

Before I can answer, we hear my name screamed through the graveyard. Someone must have told my mom about all my sneaking around.

"Alma! Alma! You come here right this minute."

Leonor's face turns beet red. My heart skips a beat. We both look toward the entrance to the graveyard and see my mom running toward us.

"Come on!" Leonor says. She looks like she's never been in trouble before.

Maybe she hasn't ever been in trouble before.

Maybe I taught her to lie and sneak to graveyards. The same things I taught Julia.

I follow behind her slowly.

As soon as she can reach me, my mom grabs my wrist and yanks me so that I'm standing next to her. She towers over me. "Do you want to explain to me what you're doing in this graveyard when you are supposed to be studying Portuguese at school?" she demands.

Every other time she's towered over me, I've cowered beneath her. Every other time I've been afraid. But that's because my heart was open. That's because I was standing there aching for love. Now my heart is closed and I know my mom was at least as wrong as I was. So I stand up straight.

"I think Adam already told you," I say. "That's how you found me, isn't it?"

Leonor is quiet next to me. She stares at her shoes.

"Thank goodness Adam told me," Mom says. "You two are too young to be running around by yourselves without anyone knowing where you are."

"I guess Adam only keeps your secrets," I say.

Leonor breathes a small gasp at my rudeness.

"Alma Meredith McArthur!" Mom says, like I'm a tiny kid. Usually this is where I would be shrinking. Today my closed-up heart keeps me my rightful size.

She doesn't say anything else, just yanks me toward the trolley. Leonor follows.

Once we're seated with her hand still clutching my wrist so tight it may bruise, she says, "It's going to take me a long time to think about a consequence for this one. I took you to Portugal. I gave you the best adventure a kid could ask for. And here you are sneaking around and lying. You have broken my trust big-time."

I snort. It's a laugh-snort. Somehow in the middle of my life falling apart, I'm laughing.

"Don't you laugh, young lady," Mom says.

I laugh again.

"What's so funny?" Mom asks.

I raise my eyebrows. She's asking me a question in the middle of a lecture. I must be breaking her.

"You said trust," I say. "You said *I* have broken *your* trust."

"What's that supposed to mean?" Mom says.

I take a minute. I don't know what she knows that I know at this point but I do know that this whole chain of knowing and not-knowing isn't all her fault. Not completely.

Mom says nothing else the entire way back to our apartment.

I don't care.

I don't care that her bun is wrapped tighter than ever and her lips are pulled into such a deep line her mouth looks like one big wrinkle.

Right now, I don't care if she loves me.

Right now, I don't care if anyone does.

As soon as we're in the hallway of our apartment and out of Leonor's hearing distance, she starts talking again. "Alma, I am incredibly disappointed in you," she says. She follows me into the kitchen, where I put my bag on the table and hang my sweater on the chair. "I cannot believe you would sneak around this way."

She's repeating herself.

I let her words wash right over my head. I don't even hear them. They don't apply anymore. She can't yell at me for sneaking and lying. I learned it all from her.

She puts her phone down on the table.

"You had better start explaining," she says.

I walk toward her. Then I pick up the phone and walk right past her.

"Alma!" she says. "Alma! I don't think so!"

But I'm already dialing.

"You are grounded from the phone, young lady," Mom says. "You're grounded from everything."

But it's already ringing.

"It's too bad for Julia because it's not her fault but you are grounded from all electronics until further notice."

But I'm not calling Julia.

When Nanny picks up I ask right away. It would usually be harder to ask my questions. It would be hard to ignore all the memories of cooking with her in the kitchen and the drawer she kept full of crayons just for me. Today, I open my mouth and the question comes easily.

"Why did you tell me my dad was dead when he's actually alive?"

My mom gasps behind me. She puts her hand down and stops reaching for the phone.

"Hello, Alma," Nanny says. "It's nice to hear from you." She speaks evenly, as if I'd only asked about the weather. She doesn't let me know at all if she heard me.

Something is connecting in my head. It's like bells are ringing.

"Would you put your mother on the phone, please?" she says.

My mother has frozen behind me in the hallway. She's frozen.

Scared, I realize.

She's scared of Nanny.

Instead of handing her the phone, I pull it away from my ear and turn on the speakerphone.

"Hi, Mom," Mom says. "I'm sorry about this. We're having a bit of a day here, as you can tell."

"Mercy," Nanny says, the same way my mom just said "Alma" in the graveyard a few minutes ago. "I told you she was too young. I told you she wasn't ready for this trip."

My jaw drops.

Mom lunges for the phone. I hold it away from her.

"I told you she was too young to know her dad was nothing but a deadbeat."

"Mom," my mom says. "Stop."

"You'd better come up with an explanation for that little girl," Nanny says. "She shouldn't have to deal with this. It wasn't her fault her parents got irresponsible and had a kid so young. It wasn't her fault. And she shouldn't have to know it all. She's too young."

"Mom!" my mom says.

"I'm not too young, Nanny," I say.

"Alma!" Nanny says, shocked. "I thought you gave your mother the phone."

"You're on speaker," I say. "And I met my dad, Nanny. I wish I knew about him all along. Even the bad stuff. I wish I hadn't spent so long mourning a person who was alive."

"Alma, now you hang up the phone. You're turning into a sneaky kid just like your mom was."

I look at my mom's face. Her eyebrows are raised and her mouth is open like she wants to say something but her words aren't coming. She looks shocked and panicked, the way I often feel around her.

Connections zip between us like electric currents: from my brain to my mom's brain to Nanny on the phone. I see it so clearly.

Nanny says my mom was a sneaky kid.

But that's because Nanny is sneaky.

And now I've become a sneaky kid.

And Nanny was probably a sneaky kid.

And if I don't stop this, our whole family will be an electrical chain of sneaky kids.

"You met him?" Mom whispers behind me.

"Didn't Adam tell you?" I whisper back.

I turn to look at her. She shakes her head. "Not that part," she says. There are tears in her eyes. Nanny is still talking about how irresponsible Mom has been to let me have this, this one teaspoon of my dad.

"Mom," my mom says. "Alma's right. She's ready. We're

going to hang up now so that I can tell her the truth."

She reaches for the phone. This time I let her. She hangs up.

Then she walks into the kitchen and sits on the couch.

"Come on, sweetie," she says to me. "This is going to take a while."

twenty-five
WHAT IF I HAVE QUESTIONS?

MOM PUTS HER ARM AROUND ME. I settle into her. I'll give her that, my shoulders and back, in exchange for finally, *finally* getting the truth.

But the first words out of her mouth form a question.

"How did you find him?" she asks.

"No," I say. "No. You go first. You tell me. Everything. Then I'll talk."

Mom swallows. She opens her mouth then closes it again. She makes her eyes do that weepy thing.

I won't let myself feel bad for her.

"You have to," I say.

"What do you want to know?" Mom asks.

"I want to know everything. The answers to all the questions I've been asking my whole life!" I exclaim.

Mom looks down at her feet.

When she doesn't say anything, I say, "Why? Why did you

let me think he was dead?"

Mom sighs. "I have to back up to explain that," she says.

"Then back up," I say. "Back up and tell me the whole thing."

"OK," she says. "Here goes." She takes a deep breath. "When I was in college, I majored in the romance languages."

"What?" I say. "What does this have to do with anything?"

Mom shakes her head. "Alma, I'm going to try to tell you this story. The story of you. Of how you came to be and how we became a family. But I don't know how to do it. So I may stumble a little. You're going to have to stay quiet and listen."

"But what if I have questions?" I say.

Mom smiles. "Let's leave all questions until the end of the story, OK?"

Those words swirl through my ear canal and into my brain. They do a happy tap dance on my brain cells.

Let's leave all questions until the end of the story.

That's the best answer to a Bad Question my mom has ever given me.

She tells me the story.

"I was studying in Portugal for my junior year of college. I was nineteen years old, only seven years older than you are now. I was young. I was supposed to spend the first semester in Portugal and the second semester in Paris. Instead, I met Jorge."

She goes on with the story, telling me they met in art class and he was funny and sweet. They would spend mornings drinking espresso at the local bakery and eating pastéis de nata. They would paint together in the afternoons. She says pretty soon she fell in love and then suddenly she was pregnant.

"With me," I say.

Mom nods. "And then everything changed. I changed everything. For you. I changed my whole life for you."

My mom had to do more than leave Portugal and skip a semester in Paris. She had to come home and drop out of college. She ended up finishing college online, but only after I was a few years old.

She had to move back in with Nanny and PopPop because she didn't have a job and she didn't know how to raise a kid.

"Nanny and PopPop were all I had," Mom says. "I had to listen to them. I had to get my act together. I couldn't just drink coffee and paint all day the way I used to. I needed to be a grown-up. For you. I got organized. I wrote lists. I followed routines so that I could take care of you and make sure you had enough sleep and food and the right sort of educational toys. I had to grow up in an instant. And I only had Nanny and PopPop to support me."

"You started wearing your hair in a bun," I say. My heart is sinking. It's so low it might slip out onto the couch.

I'm thinking about all the stuff I forced her to give up. Paris. College. The chance to grow up on her own without having to do everything Nanny and PopPop said.

Mom must notice somehow or something. "Alma," she says. "Sweetie. You were worth it. You were always totally, completely worth it. For all of us."

My heart wiggles a little. Maybe some of the roads are starting to open.

"And my . . . and Jorge?" I say.

"Jorge was . . . he wanted to . . . Alma, I don't want to speak for him. I'll just tell you what happened. He agreed I had to move back to Pittsburgh with my parents and he said he'd be there right after me. He even filled out some job applications for work in the States. I saw him do it.

"But then I moved home to Pennsylvania and I had you. Then Nanny and PopPop moved to Florida and I had no choice but to follow them."

"OH!" I say. "That's why it says I was born in Pennsylvania on my birth certificate even though my first memories are in Florida."

Mom lowers her eyebrows. "That part I would have always explained to you," she says.

"But you didn't," I say.

Mom shakes her head. "Anyway, Jorge never came. I wrote to him all the time. For a while he said he'd come soon. In the next six months. He'd promise. He made so many promises. First Nanny and PopPop stopped believing him. Then I did too. He kept saying that he was coming when you were six months old, a year, eighteen months."

"Wow," I whisper. "He never even met me."

All these years I've been imagining my dad as this perfect

person. In real life, he never even met me.

"I didn't think I could tell you that you had this sort of dad. One who won't do anything for you. I don't know, Alma. He sent you a little stuffed lion when you turned two. And then that was it. The next thing I knew, you were asking Nanny about him and she told you . . . Well, you know."

"Why did you let her do that though?"

Mom shrugs. "What else could I have done?" she asks.

I turn to look at her. Her eyes look more open than they ever have. Her bun is loose and sagging. It's time for the truth. For both of us.

"You should have told me," I say.

"Told you what?" Mom asks.

"The truth," I say.

"Alma!" Mom says. "You were four years old. You were just a little girl."

"So?" I say.

"So," Mom says. "I couldn't look into your little eyes and break your heart. I couldn't tell you your dad knew about you but didn't do anything for you. I couldn't tell you he disappeared."

"Why not?" I ask.

Mom shakes her head.

"It would hurt too much," she says. "It would hurt you too much."

"Mom," I say. The word is salty. I realize there are tears.

There are tears on both of our faces. "How old did you think I would have to be so that it wouldn't hurt so much? Because it hurts pretty badly now."

"Oh, Alma," Mom says. Then she opens her arms and I fall into them.

"I never stopped writing to him," Mom says. "I never gave up hope that he'd someday get his act together for you. But when Adam asked you that question, the one about . . ."

She can't seem to say it. "I know which one," I say.

"When he asked that, I realized that Jorge was one thing. Consistent. Consistently gone. He was never going to show up for you. And if I ever wanted you to understand the truth, I had to take you to see him. To find out for yourself."

"Why?" I ask, muffled into her shoulder. "Why wouldn't he . . ."

She doesn't need me to use the rest of the words.

"Baby, he says he'll be at the family gathering this weekend. I'll have Flávia check in with him again now that you've seen and talked to him, but before he was saying he would be there. So, when you see him there, you ask him. You ask him why he disappeared. You don't let him walk away until he's answered. I couldn't tell you. It's been the biggest mystery of my life. Every day I look at you and I wonder what the heck he was thinking. But I will say this. This is the biggest truth I know. He missed out. You are perfect. He missed out. He missed everything."

It's bigger than the speck of truth I used to have.

The truth that he loved me.

It's more true too. I'll lean on this piece of truth from now on.

He missed out. He missed everything.

twenty-six
WHERE WOULD WE BE WITHOUT MY MOM?

MOM LETS ME STAY HOME FROM school the next day. She calls it "Emotional Exhaustion Personal Day."

Mom still won't say what I want her to. What I need her to. I want her to say, "You're right. I should have told you."

And I'm still sad. Sadder than sad. I'm grieving the dad that I thought I was burying notes for. I'm grieving the dad I did find who thought it was OK to go away after a month of guitar and video games. I'm grieving the mom my mom could have maybe been if she'd gotten a chance to grow up a little bit more before becoming a mom. And I'm grieving the dad I should have had. The one who went away and stopped telling me the truth. The one who will never be more than ex-stepdad now.

I spend the day trying to Skype Julia. It's always tough with the time difference, but I'm not going to school so I can try the entire day. At home it's the first day of fall break. I know she'll pick up eventually.

It's been too long since we talked.

And the last time we did, I told her a lie. I told her I'd found my dad dead and buried. I told her he was humble and responsible and all sorts of other things I wanted him to be.

I don't want to tell her the truth. I sort of want her to keep thinking of my dad as this humble superstar buried under the earth. But I know if I let Julia think that, I maybe will also let all my friends think that. And then maybe I'll let my own kids think that.

I have to start telling the truth now.

But all day long Skype rings and rings. Julia never answers.

I go down to avó's apartment when Leonor gets home from school. I play piano with avó for a little while, then I sit on her couch with my cousin and I tell her what my mom told me. It feels weird to talk like this, loudly and openly, in front of avó. But I don't want to sneak around and hide things anymore. I think avó can see how sad I am, how much of my story was stolen from me.

Of course this is an easy way to practice honesty considering avó doesn't speak English. Still. Leonor says "Tio Jorge" enough that I know she has some sense of what we're talking about.

"He didn't want me," I say. "That's the end of it. That's why he disappeared. Twice."

Leonor thinks for a minute. She taps her fingers along the

bumps on the braid on the back of her head. "But that doesn't explain why he disappeared from everyone," she says.

Suddenly avó is next to me, her hand on mine. "É por isso que sempre serei tão grato à tua mãe," she says. I try hard to make my brain work fast enough to translate but she's already speaking again. "Olha o quão bonita és. Quão amável e inteligente e maravilhosa."

"What?" I say to Leonor.

I only know a few of the words.

Mãe = mother

Porquê = why

Olha = look

"She says she's grateful to your mom," Leonor says.

"My mom?" I say, shocked. I figured avó and Leonor would hate my mom.

"She says you turned out beautiful and kind and smart and wonderful."

My cheeks burn. I look at my grandmother. Her face is red behind her wrinkles. She really sees all of that in me? In my mom?

"Tell her my mom never told me. Tell her my mom lied."

Leonor says something in Portuguese and avó squeezes my hands and looks into my eyes and says something back.

"She says of course your mother isn't perfect. No one is. She says being a mother is hard, the hardest thing, and that your mom had to figure it out so young. Of course she made some mistakes. But that you turned out to be such a smart and thoughtful and talented and lovely girl, and we're so grateful to have you. She says your mother was doing the best she could in an impossible situation and she certainly did better than Jorge. Jorge never ever told avó your mom was in touch. Not until your mom finally reached out a few months ago."

Avó squeezes my hands again. I look between Leonor and avó. Once. Twice. Again.

"Avó's right too," Leonor says. "Someone else would have maybe never taken you here to meet us. Then where would we be?"

I can't imagine it. A few months ago I didn't know so much family could ever exist. Now I can't imagine life without them.

When I go home that night, I'm certain I'll have a message from Julia. But no. Nothing. Did she find out I lied to her? Is she mad at me?

I try to pay attention in school the next day, but it's nearly impossible. Tomorrow is a school holiday and in two days I'll be meeting the rest of my aunts, uncles, and cousins. And maybe my dad will come back. Both Mom and avó warned me that he may not actually show up. I know he doesn't have a great track record for that sort of thing . . . showing up. But if I do see him, I know I'll be able to ask the questions I have to ask. I'll be able to demand the answers. Finally.

When I get home, Mom is in her room speaking English for once. That's strange but I don't bother to think about it.

Instead I dive across my too-low double bed and grab my tablet. I click Skype.

Just seeing Julia's icon on the screen makes my tongue tickle with everything I have to tell her.

But she doesn't pick up.

She has to be home today. It's fall break at home.

Pick up, pick up, pick up, I beg her across the ocean.

I try again.

No answer.

She's mad at me.

I wonder if she'll ever forgive me.

Is this how she finally disappears?

I remember what I told her last time. How I looked right at her through the screen and told her a lie. I did the same thing my mother had done to me for years. I even told her the exact same lie. I can't be that person. I have to fix it. Now.

She's mad at me and she should be. It's all my fault.

I picture her face filling the screen. I imagine the way she'll say "Alma!" like my name is even better than "hello."

I'll manifest her into my tablet.

I click the icon again. It rings. And then "Alma!"

Except her face isn't on the screen. The tablet is still ringing. And the voice is coming from behind me.

I turn, tears already in my eyes. And there she is, all five feet of her standing in the doorway to my bedroom.

Not mad at me.

Not disappeared.

She's here. She's *here*.

"Alma!" she says again. "Happy fall break!"

"Ju—" I try to say her name back but I can't get the word out of my mouth. Instead I rush at her. She rushes back at me and we hug so hard we fall over onto the bed.

Before we're even done hugging, I say it. "I didn't tell you the truth. I need to tell you something."

But then two grown-ups are laughing at us. We look up.

My mom.

And next to her . . . someone else who could have disappeared.

Someone else who didn't.

Adam.

The sight of him is blinding, like staring right into the sun. I swallow three times quickly so I don't start crying.

"Hi, Alma-bear," he says.

Something shifts in my heart as I hug all three of them over and over. Something loosens just a little. A tiny inroad opens again.

We're all out to dinner at the restaurant Mom and I went to one of the first nights we were here. Julia sits on one side of me, Mom on the other. Adam is at the head of the table next to Julia, avó sits next to Mom. Leonor sits across from us.

I still have the lie I told climbing up my throat. I'm desperate to get Julia alone. I can't explain it in front of all these people.

But Julia and I cannot stop giggling. Nothing is funny. It's not a funny-giggle. It's just the joy of her next to me bubbling up in my lungs and jumping through my throat. The adults all seem annoyed by it but I'm checking on Leonor out of the corner of my eye and she's smiling. I hope she knows Julia and I aren't trying to leave her out. There are just no words to explain why we're giggling.

"So you aren't angry with me?" Julia asks when the food comes.

"Angry with you?" I say. How could I possibly be angry?

"I know you don't like secrets," Julia says. It's loud enough for my mom to hear. But I think I'm done worrying what she thinks. I don't care if she's listening.

"This isn't a secret!" I say. "It's a surprise!"

"What's the difference?" Julia asks.

"A secret is forever. Someone is never supposed to find out. A surprise is temporary."

"Goodness, that's true!" Leonor says.

"Wait a minute," I say, turning to Mom and avó. "What about everyone else?"

"Who else?" Mom asks.

"All the aunts and uncles and cousins that are supposed to come on Saturday. I thought this was family weekend."

"It is," Mom says. "Look around. This is your family right here."

I do, and in a way she's right. Except for Nanny and PopPop,

I think all the people who care the most about me are sitting around this table.

Mom keeps talking. "Everyone is still coming Saturday," she says. "But when Adam called me to let me know some of what's been going on with you, he asked if maybe he could come and visit. He didn't want you to forget that there have always been, and will always be, people who love you. And he was right, so of course I said he should come right away. And then we thought it might be even better if he brought Julia with him."

"Uncle Adam convinced my mom to let me spend fall break here with you!" Julia says.

"Julia and Adam can be with you when you meet your entire family. And me of course. So you have some support if you get overwhelmed or sad," Mom says.

Adam smiles.

My mouth drops open. I'm so shocked she said that. She knows I might get sad. And it would be OK if I do.

"But . . . But I'm supposed to be in trouble," I say.

Mom nods. "You are," she says. "I'm still incredibly disappointed that you snuck out and spent so many days with me not knowing where you were. I have to think about how I can trust you again now. But also, sometimes children need love more than punishment." Mom looks at Adam. "We figured this was one of those times."

I stare at her. I think about all the lies she told me. I think about all the hours I spent searching graveyards for a man who was alive on the other side of the world. I think about all the questions she refused to answer. I'm still in trouble and I'm also still mad at her. But maybe I can do that too. I can choose love over anger. Just for tonight.

By the time dinner is over, Julia is yawning. She's barely finished with one yawn before the next one starts. Adam puts his arm around Julia for the walk home and I think Julia might fall asleep standing up.

"Jet lag," Adam says over her head. Then he reaches over and pulls me into her other side. It's a weird feeling, being this close to him for the first time in months. He smells different now that he doesn't live in our old house. He smells like sunscreen and fresh rain. He feels different too.

"So, kiddo, how are you liking Portugal?" he asks. Adam always asked me questions.

"It's beautiful but . . . it's been hard," I say. The truth. I tell the truth from now on.

Adam squeezes my shoulders. "I know, baby. You've been so strong."

Julia manages to lift her head for a second to peek at me. Soon we will be alone in my room and I can tell her the truth about Jorge.

But I don't get to tell her. Julia falls into my bed and is asleep within one minute of us getting back to our tiny apartment.

I curl up in bed next to my best friend. And I say a little prayer that she'll wake up early so that I can tell her everything.

Julia's shaking me awake before the sun is up. Mom is snoring lightly on the other side of the wall. Adam is asleep on the couch in the kitchen. Still I put on music softly so that if they did wake up they wouldn't be able to hear us.

And then we sit side by side on top of my unmade bed, our pj-ed legs kicked out in front of us.

I say, "I want to tell you about my dad. Is that OK now?"

Julia hops up so that she's sitting on her feet. "Did you find out more about him?" she asks. "Will you take me to see his grave today? I know I complained about spending so much time in graveyards but now I'd really like to see it."

"Julia . . . I'm so sorry. I lied to you. I lied because my mom lied and her mom lied and I have to figure out a way to stop lying after spending the first twelve years of my life living in lies."

Julia tilts her head. "Huh?"

"He doesn't have a grave."

Julia's eyes go wide. "My mom was right?" she whispers.

I freeze. "What do you mean?"

"My mom always said she thinks maybe he's still alive. Maybe that's why there are so many secrets."

"So your mom didn't know?" I say.

"Well, she thought maybe," Julia says.

"No, I mean . . . I mean . . . Your mom didn't just not tell me. She couldn't. She didn't know."

"Not tell you what, Alma? That your father's alive? She wouldn't do that. No good person would do that."

I swallow. I guess that makes Mom and Adam not-good people.

Julia tries to recover for a minute. "I mean . . . not good people, but. You know what I mean. Like. My mom. She would have told you."

"I know," I say.

Julia is quiet a second, then bouncing again. "Wait!" she says. "We're missing the important part. He's alive? How did you find out? Have you met him?"

I raise one eyebrow and nod. Then I tell her the whole story. I end with the part where he was teaching me guitar chords.

"So . . ." Julia whispers. "Do I get to meet him?"

I take a deep breath. I realize I still haven't told her the whole story. I've made him seem fun with all the video games and guitars. Telling the truth is harder than I thought.

"Maybe," I say. "Mom says he said he'd be at the family reunion thing tomorrow . . . But when I saw him last, he told me that was all he had to give me. A month of hanging out in a graveyard. He said that was all he had to offer."

"Oh, Alma," Julia says.

She reaches to put her arms around me but I scoot backward. I feel sort of icky, like all the not-good people in my life are piled onto my skin like dirt.

"Guess I ended up with three not-good parents," I say.

"Hold on," Julia says. Then she gets up and walks out of the room.

I'm left on the bed with my mouth hanging open, dumbfounded.

But Julia's back quickly. "I was just making sure your mom was still sleeping," she says. She walks over to her suitcase and pulls something out. "I have to show you something."

She puts a purple folder, one like we'd use at school, on the bed. When she flips it open, I just see a bunch of documents and typed paper. Most is in English, but there are some Korean characters too.

"What is this?" I ask.

Julia's voice is the quietest it could possibly be. "My adoption papers," she says.

"Your mom doesn't know you have these?"

She shakes her head. "I guess my mom isn't always a good person either," she says. "I mean, she is to you. Because she understands your family. She gets that you miss your dad. You're supposed to. But me . . . I think I'm not supposed to even want to see these."

"That's messed up, Jules," I say. "She had all this stuff and she kept it from you?"

Julia shrugs. "She said she'd tell me when I'm in high school. But I thought I might explode by then. It's still not enough, really. I figured out the orphanage I was in. I looked it up online but all I could find really was a Google Earth photo. I want to know what it was like over there. What I was doing. You know?"

I scoot closer to her and put my arm around her, but she shrugs it off. I understand.

"I want to know what it looked like when I looked out the window. I want to know what I ate and what songs I learned to sing. I want to be able to read this." She points to a paragraph on her papers written in Korean.

"But I'm like not supposed to care about this, you know? I mean, I ended up with great parents. I should just be happy. I don't know what's wrong with me."

"Nothing's wrong with you!" I say.

Julia shudders. "I can't stop thinking about her. Like, is she alive?"

"Julia," I say. "That's normal."

"Does she think about me? Is she safe? Does she have other kids? Does she still talk to my dad? Do they ever talk about me?"

Julia is distressed but with each of her questions the weight on my shoulders gets lighter and lighter.

"I never knew you had so many questions," I say.

"It's like I'm made of questions," Julia says. "It's like all I am is questions."

I smile at her. "That's why we're best friends. It's the same for me too."

She smiles back at me, a little bit of friendship peeking

through her sadness. I love how that can happen when you have a best friend. "But you have answers now."

"Exactly," I say, smiling. "Which means I have more time to try to find some for you."

"We don't have to," Julia says. "I'm supposed to be grate—"

"Julia!" I interrupt her. "You know what? I should be grateful too. My mom gave up an entire life to raise me the right way. And she did so many things right. I always had clothes and food and piano lessons and soccer games and help with homework . . . But . . . I still missed my dad."

Julia nods.

"I think you can be grateful, but you shouldn't have to be. You're supposed to have a family. Every kid deserves one. And no matter how you feel, you can still miss your mom."

Julia thinks for a minute. "Maybe you're right," she says.

"Open the folder again."

Julia lowers her eyebrows. "Are you sure? Don't we need to do things today? Like to get ready for your family and everything?"

"No," I say. "That will be hard enough tomorrow. Julia, today this is about you."

twenty-seven
WILL HE SHOW UP?

LATER THAT DAY, MOM SENDS JULIA into the shower and calls me into her room. After spending the morning poring over Julia's papers and attempting to Google Translate all the Korean, we still haven't found out that much.

Julia is going to have to talk to her parents about it.

I'm going to have to give her a lesson in the truth.

Mom spreads photo albums on her bed. They are old and dusty and I'm pretty sure they came from avó's apartment.

"I want to give you an idea of who everyone is before tomorrow."

"OK," I say. I go sit on her bed. I shiver.

The truth is that I'm still angry with her. I need to tell her that. I need real answers. I can't choose love over anger every day. Sometimes they exist together, in the same room, coming from the same place.

She starts pointing to pictures. "This is your uncle Gregoria and your aunt Mariana and your cousins Gasper and Paulo and Ana. Of course they are a little older now. This is not exactly an up-to-date photo album."

I'm barely listening to her. I'm thinking about all the times she let me believe that he was dead. That he was in a graveyard. That he died of some disease sort of like cancer. They were all lies.

I don't know how to let that go so quickly.

Someone knocks on the door. Mom gets up and opens it. Adam comes in behind her.

Adam who also let me believe a lie. Adam who didn't save me when he could have.

Mom walks over to the photo album and I don't want to hear about one more relative from her when these lies are still hanging between us.

"You both should have told me," I say.

"Alma, sweetie, you know we couldn't," Mom says, voice up and down and up and down.

At the same time, Adam says, "I know. I should have."

"Adam!" Mom says. "You couldn't tell her. I hadn't told her yet."

Adam leans against the door. He crosses one foot in front of the other. "You know I always went with that, Mercy, until the other day when Alma called. I mean, I always thought you were right. It wasn't my place to tell her. She's your daughter."

There's a tiny difference in the voices grown-ups use when they talk to each other instead of talking to a kid. I've heard

Adam's voice like this before but only when I was listening in on something I wasn't supposed to hear. When he talks now, in his grown-up voice, about things I said, it makes me feel big and important and in charge of my own brain and my own worries.

I wish more than ever that he really was my dad.

"But Alma brought up a good point," Adam says. "She said if I wanted to adopt her, I should have told her. I was ready to be her dad so I should have stood up for what I knew was right. Instead I let a lie keep hurting and hurting her." He looks at me. "Alma, I'm sorry. I hope you'll forgive me."

I thought the apology would feel better than it does. But I nod anyway.

Then Adam comes and sits on the floor at my feet. He reaches up and takes one of my hands.

"And that's not all, Alma-bear," he says. "I'm sorry for everything else too. For leaving and for not calling until you called me. I'm sorry for giving you another reason to be sad. That time I saw you at Julia's house and it was so awkward when it should have been joyful. I was just so . . ." He looks at Mom. "Well, this is the truth. I was heartbroken. I missed you both so much. But that doesn't make it OK. I was ready to be your dad and instead I left you? It makes me sick to my stomach when I realize how it must have looked to you."

I'm crying now. This apology is much better.

"But I'm not going to do it again. And I hope you'll give me another chance."

"Another chance?" I blubber. "At being my dad?"

Adam smiles a half smile, a sad one. He glances at Mom, who is keeping her eyes on her feet.

"Well, maybe not officially," Adam says. "But I'd like to do what I can to fill that role. I'm going to come back to Portugal for Christmas to see you. And when you move back home—"

"Move back home?" I say. "We're moving back home?"

Mom chuckles. "Did you think I was going to bring you here forever? We're only here for a year."

"Why only for a year?" I ask.

"I thought you deserved a chance to really live here. To understand the food and the culture and the language. To really get to know your grandmother and your family. To maybe give Jorge a few chances. But we can't stay here forever."

I look at her again, keeping my eyes steady to show I'm serious. "You should have told me that," I say.

Mom scrunches up her nose. "Well, I didn't know if you'd want to leave after a year. And I didn't know if you'd be hoping to go home sooner. And I didn't know how to . . ." She pauses and looks at me. "You know what. You're right, Alma. I should have told you."

I take a deep breath. I suck those words into my lungs. I hold them there. This might be the closest I ever get to an apology and I have to savor it.

"When you do come home," Adam says. "Your mother said maybe you can spend some time at my house too? Maybe one weekend a month?"

My jaw drops. That sounds like a dad. One weekend a month. Holidays. It's like a regular divorced dad.

I doubt kids are usually happy when their parents talk about how their time will be split up after divorce, but to me this feels amazing.

"Sounds good," I say.

"Really?" Adam says. His face has the smile my heart wants my face to have. But I don't want to give that to him and Mom yet. I'm still too angry.

"Shall we go back to the pictures?" Mom says.

I shake my head. "I can't learn that way," I say. "And anyway, the only person I really want to see is Jorge."

"Really?" Mom says.

I nod. "I have some questions to ask him."

"Alma, sweets," she says. She puts her arm around me. "I know that. And Flávia said she called him yesterday and he's still saying he'll be there. But he doesn't come around the family very often. She warned me he doesn't always show up where he promises. I don't think I can guarantee that he'll be there."

"I know," I say. "But I can hope. And don't tell me not to. I'm going to do what my heart says to do even if you think I'm too young for it."

Mom smiles. "OK," she says. "I can respect that."

I wait with Julia on the stairs outside our apartment building. The rest of my family is gathering in a restaurant. Apparently avó has an in with some restaurant owner and they closed down the place so that we could all be together today. We're leaving in just a little bit. I'm nervous for what I'm going to say to Jorge if he comes. I'm nervous that maybe he won't come.

Julia is sitting next to me so our shoulders are touching, the way we used to sit together as little girls. She's singing Taylor Swift and I'm trying to sing along because she's right that a little Tay-Tay is basically the only thing that could take my mind off this right now, but even that isn't helping very much.

I interrupt her to tell her about the new plan with Adam when I get home.

"He's adopting you?" she asks. "He can do that?"

"Well, no," I say. "Not officially."

"Are you going to call him dad?" Julia asks.

I close my eyes and think about it. I want to. I want him to remember that he made these promises to me every time he talks to me. I want to use the word as a guarantee that he won't disappear again. "I think so," I say.

"Sounds close enough to me," Julia says. She bumps her shoulder against mine. "We'll both be adopted."

I smile at her.

Then her eyes get wide. "Alma!" she says. She throws her arms around me. "Your dad will be my uncle. . . . We'll be cousins!"

"Oh yeah!" I say, squeezing her back. My heart bounces around my chest with joy. Who knew I could feel joy while at the same time being so worried.

But the joy is real. Two new cousins in two months.

The two best cousins a girl could have.

It almost makes me feel lucky.

I was hoping to find a grave in this country. I didn't. Instead I got one dad, one grandmother, and two cousins. That should be enough.

Mom comes down the stairs behind us. Adam follows her.

"Ready, girls?" Mom says. "Flávia and Leonor are already there."

"Ready," Julia says.

I get up and follow.

As we walk the winding pathways of the old part of the city, I try to stay as close to Adam as possible. Even if Jorge has terrible answers, I'll have a dad at the end of this. Even if Jorge isn't there, I'll have a dad at the end of this.

It's funny how I sort of know my way around now. I know that when we turn this corner there will be a set of stairs and a huge mural with a priest hanging out of a window and a woman at a table eating bread with a big glass of wine. I know that if we turn another corner there will be cars because we'll be back on the road again despite an imperceptible difference in the size of the streets. It feels like I know Lisbon about as well as I know myself now. Still twists and turns and lots of surprises. But I'm getting more confident that I can navigate it.

We reach the little restaurant nestled into one of the walls behind a set of stairs. There are three big windows in the front. I see shadowed figures moving around them. I stop walking. My heart is pounding so fast my legs can't move at the same time.

Adam, Mom, and Julia take a few more steps before realizing they've left me behind.

Julia walks back and takes my hand. "Come on," she says. "You can do this."

I nod and walk with her to the door of the restaurant. Mom and Adam pause behind us.

I see people moving in all directions. There's cheerful music playing. There's a buffet set up in a corner. Some people are standing around chatting. Some are playing on the floor with small children and babies. Some are in line for food or sitting at one of the tables eating.

I look and look for him. I scan each face.

He's not at the tables. He's not on the floor. He's not chatting in the corner.

He's not here.

I turn to look at the three people I have. The three who are no way nohow disappearing. "He's not here," I say.

Mom frowns and her eyes get that weepy look in them. "Alma," she says. I know she wants to tell me not to care. I know she wants to tell me to just have a good time. But she doesn't. She stops.

"He's not," Adam says. "You must be disappointed."

I nod.

My heart aches for him. Somehow my heart is aching for

the actual Jorge. The one who only plays guitar and video games and complains about work. The one who has only ever given me a small stuffed lion and a pastel de nata. The one who said a month was "enough." He wasn't the dad I always dreamed of, but still, he was my dad.

"I think I'm always going to miss him," I say out loud. I tell the truth now in this moment when it would be so much easier to put on a fake smile.

"I know," Adam says. "You will. But look." He points through the door at all the people who are my aunts and uncles and cousins, my family I've never met. "You do have all these people who traveled here to meet you. To see you. You can miss your dad and get to know them too."

I look up at him. I look at Julia. I look at my mom.

I know they aren't who he meant. But they all traveled here, across the ocean, to be here for me. They are all standing in this doorway, still, waiting for me to be ready.

No matter how many new aunts and uncles and cousins and grandmothers I get. No matter how many more people I start to love. No matter how different life gets. I'll have them.

Family.

Turn the page for a sneak peek at Caela Carter's
next poignant and timely novel . . .

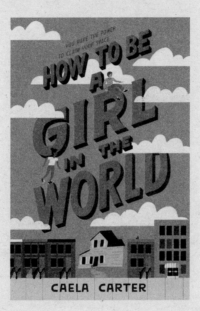

CHAPTER 1

OUR HEADS TILT ONE AT A time. Mine. Mom's. Emma's. Like raindrops falling in a row. *Tilt. Tilt. Tilt.*

We're standing on the sidewalk, holding hands and staring at a ramshackle house in front of us. The entire thing looks like it's leaning onto its right side. Like it had a really tough day of work and is standing in the station, waiting for the subway, resting against one of those poles that Mom always tells me is disgusting and I should never touch.

"It's not tilted," Mom says, reading our minds. Or our heads. She's talking too fast, the way she does when it's really important that I agree with her. It's hard to agree with whatever this is. "It only looks like it's leaning because there's an extra window on the left side. Asymmetrical windows. That's why this didn't sell. Can you believe it? Well, it sold!"

Mom has bought this house. The tilting-but-not-tilting house.

I don't think asymmetrical windows were ever this house's only problem. It's set back a few feet from the street, as if there's room for a yard or a driveway or something, but all that's in front of it is dirty, cracked sidewalk concrete. It has a front stoop made of bricks, like most of the houses in our Brooklyn neighborhood. But the rest of the house is a faded green color, as close as green could get to white. Instead of brick or stone, it's covered in aluminum siding, and there are places where the siding is sliding off. There are poles for an awning over the front porch, but the awning is gone, if it was ever there. And there is exactly one shutter on each window, except the asymmetrical one, which has two. Which maybe makes it look even more asymmetrical.

Mom says we are going to live here. I scrunch up my eyebrows and tell my brain to imagine it. I can't.

"Can you believe I scooped this up before someone decided to flip it?" She keeps talking, but she's answering the wrong questions. "I mean, it's incredible. And I know the neighborhood's a little rough, but we're less than a ten-minute walk from our apartment now, so it can't be that different, right? Just a slightly longer ride to school for you girls. You probably won't have to worry about that until springtime anyway."

"I won't still be living with you in spring," Emma says, like always.

Mom shrugs, like always. "We'll see."

Then she's talking about rent versus mortgage and Catholic school tuition and the value of ownership and all sorts of things I don't care about. I hate when she talks about money.

I only have one question right now: Does this tilted house have air-conditioning?

I should have a trillion questions, I know that. Until five minutes ago I didn't know we were moving at all. There's no reason to move, really, except Mom says renting is a waste and she's always wanted to be able to buy a house. I should be wondering why this house. Why now.

But the sweat trickling down between my shoulder blades keeps me from thinking about anything else. It's ninety degrees outside and steam is rising from the sidewalks in sheets. This is August in Brooklyn.

I'm dressed in black sweatpants that used to be baggy but are now clinging to the sweat on my legs. I have my purple turtleneck tucked into them, the sleeves pulled all the way down, so that the only bits of my skin that are showing are on my face and hands.

Mom and Emma are both in shorts and T-shirts. When Mom saw what I was wearing this morning she sighed, but she didn't say anything. It's the end of the summer. She's as sick of telling me my outfits are crazy as I am of defending them.

But she's wrong. At least I'm covered. I'd rather be sweaty than exposed.

"Now, girls," Mom says. "We're going to have a lot to do once we get inside, OK? The previous owners left piles of possessions here, and we have to either throw it all away or donate it to charity. I'm going to need your help to get the house into shape."

Then she turns to me. She wraps her hands around mine and I have to look down slightly to focus on her. Mom is small and I've always known that but I'm still getting used to her being smaller than *me*. I look in her green eyes and forget about the sweat for just a second. These moments have been so rare in the year since Emma started living with us. The ones where Mom remembers that I'm her daughter and Emma is her niece. The ones where Mom remembers that it was me first, that it was just the two of us for a long, long time.

She puts her hand on my face, which is totally fine because she's my mom and all the extra fabric I've been wearing this summer has nothing to do with her.

"We did it, baby girl," she says. "We're homeowners."

A little bit of the excitement she's been filled up with spills into me. I smile at her. Despite the sweat, I shiver a little bit.

This is a big moment.

My mom and I own a house.

She hands me the keys. "Lydia," she says, "you do it. You open the door."

I nod and smile, then walk up the stairs to the front door. There's a huge crack in the top step. The railing is leaning so far to the left I can't even reach it.

I try to see this house the way Mom does. The way she says it will look when we're finished working on it. It's hard to see it as anything but a beat-up shack, especially considering the rows of pristine brownstones and brand-new, shiny high-rises in the neighborhood where we live. But I take a deep breath and I try.

I reach out to touch the heavy metal door in front of me. The two brass numbers fastened to it tell me our new address: 44 Washington Court. When I reach the door, one of the 4s falls off and I catch it in my palm. As I do, a *zing* goes up my arm. The 4 in my hand almost seems to talk to me.

Maybe this new house could be a good thing.

Maybe, once we move, Andrew and his friends will never know where I live.

I put my key in the front door and turn. It swings open too quickly, like it's made of Styrofoam.

Inside is a dark and dusty living room, crowded with boxes and furniture, as if someone tried to pack up but vanished halfway through the job. There's a staircase along the left wall of the living room and a doorway in the back of the living room leading to a kitchen with all the cabinets open, or maybe all the cabinet doors torn off.

A shiver goes up my spine. A good one.

I love this place. Not for the beautiful home Mom says it will become. But for its spookiness right now.

I've walked into one of the horror novels hidden under my bed. I've stepped into one of the movies my best friend, Miriam, and I love to scream at during sleepovers.

In books and movies, the answer to the problem is always in the scariest possible place. My answer is here. Somewhere hidden in this mess. I know it.

After a few hours of picking through our new creepy living room, we're walking back to our current apartment. My legs are covered. My arms are covered. My collarbone is covered. There's almost nothing left of me to look at.

As we approach our block, the chain-link fence around the park at the corner comes into view. I hear the basketballs bouncing off the backboards. I hear boys shouting. My breath catches in my throat.

Please don't look up. Please don't see me.

The boys have been at this park every day this week. I've been going to school with most of them since kindergarten, so I know they know where I live. But so far this summer they haven't bugged me when I've walked past. Maybe that's because Andrew—the worst one—has been away for the summer. Or maybe it's because I'm wearing all these clothes now.

My breath gets heavy as we walk past. *Don't look up. Don't look up.*

I rub the brass 4 from our new front door where I stashed it in my pocket. I keep pace with Mom and Emma. Then we are past them and safely inside for another day.

Our apartment looks bright and shiny with its white walls and hardwood floor and portraits of Emma and me hanging over the couch in the main room. If it weren't for the sweat and stranger-dust all over me, the whole new maybe-haunted house might feel like a dream.

"I call first shower!" Emma says, then darts into our one and only bathroom like she does every time we get home from the park or the beach or anywhere we all get sweaty. She always calls the first shower even though I'm always sweatier.

Mom raises her eyebrows at me. "It's not her fault you're dressing like it's February when it's ninety degrees outside."

"It wouldn't be fair for her to get the first shower every time even if we were dressed the same way," I say.

"She takes faster showers, Lydia," Mom says. "I need you to let this one go."

She's said that a lot since Emma moved in. It's like her mantra.

My room used to be my own—*I need you to let this one go.*

We order pizza every Friday night—*I need you to let this one go.*

You said I could get a dog when I turned twelve—*I need you to let this one go. We have Emma now.*

But Emma is not at all like the cuddly puppy I've been imagining.

I march to our room like I'm angry. But actually it's good to have a minute alone.

Emma and I have twin beds pushed up against opposite walls. I say Emma has the better side because she has the closet on hers. But the door to the room is on my side, so

7

she's always saying I have the best one. Once, Mom told us to switch but we looked at each other and started laughing.

I check to be sure I'm absolutely alone, then pull the box out from under my bed. It's just an old shoebox, so no one would ever think anything of it. But it's where I keep my notebook, and I don't ever want anyone to look at my lists and the random thoughts I use to make things make sense because ever since last spring nothing makes sense.

I take out my notebook and pencil and write a quick list:

MAGIC

I know Sister Janice and everyone at school say magic is bad, but if it's that bad then maybe it's real. Maybe it's powerful. Maybe it's what I need. Maybe our new house could be magic. Maybe these things I found in the house and took home in my pockets could also be magic.

1. The brass 4 from the front door.
2. A tiny doll the size of my thumb with gold hair and a purple dress.
3. A toilet-paper roll.

Maybe if I keep one of them in my pocket from now on, the boys . . . everyone . . . will stop bothering me.

I shove all three new objects plus my notebook into the old shoebox and slide it under the bed before Emma could possibly be done with her shower.

I know it's weird to collect strangers' things. And it's extra weird to bring home a toilet-paper roll. But the house was covered in them. There were little piles of toilet-paper rolls in every corner. I found them on the windowsills and under the couch and in the doorway to the kitchen. I found them in the kitchen cabinets and between couch cushions and behind the empty TV stand. They have to mean something.

I hear Emma turn the shower off. It's almost my turn. I know Mom will let me go next. She always goes last.

"Hey, Mom," I call. "Is it just us three for dinner?"

"Us three," Mom says, "and Jeremy is on his way too." Her voice goes up and down in a singsong way when she says *Jeremy* because he's her boyfriend and now she's in love and that's something I'm still trying to get used to for so many reasons.

I take a deep, shaky breath and shove all the words I want to say into my stomach. "OK."

When Jeremy comes for dinner he almost always sleeps over. My mom's attention has been divided ever since Emma moved in last summer. When Jeremy's here I'm down to a tiny fraction.

Plus there are other things about Jeremy. . . .

I try not to remember the way Jeremy put his hand on my shoulder and kept it there the last time I saw him when Mom wasn't home. I try not to think about how he stood two inches too close to me.

It was probably nothing.

It was probably normal.

That's what I'm telling myself as I slip the 4 into the pocket of the jeans I will put on after I shower. Just in case there's magic in anything that comes from the house. Just in case I need protecting. Just in case the scariness isn't all inside my head.

But I know it's not real. It can't be.

Mom would never choose a not-safe boyfriend.

HOW TO BECOME A WEIRDO

YOU'LL BE RUNNING AROUND THINKING YOU'RE a totally normal good girl. Your life will be filled with homework and texting and playing tag with the boys and girls at recess. The same boys and girls you've been playing tag with since kindergarten.

Then the boys will change and the girls will change and you'll be the same old you except now that same old you is a weirdo.

Andrew will give you a nickname.

Swing.

At first you won't think that much about it. Then your friend Miriam will tell you what it means. "He's calling you Swing because he likes the way your uniform skirt swings between your butt and your knees."

"What?" you'll whisper-shout. You'll feel dirty and disgusting, like bugs are crawling around your veins trying to get through your skin.

But Miriam will be telling you this in the most excited voice in the world, almost like she's forcing herself to be happy for you. Almost like she's trying with all her friendship spirit not to be jealous. So instead of crying, like you want to, you'll smile.

Soon all the boys will call you Swing.

They'll whisper things about your legs that fill you with heavy, dark, oily shame.

They'll talk about your curvy hips and how the shadow of your bra strap shows through your white uniform shirt. They'll talk about your legs and arms and shoulders and lips and chest and knees and eyes like you are just a series of different shapes.

They'll create an "invention"—a compact mirror taped on a bendy straw.

When the teacher's looking they'll pretend it's to reflect the sunlight into each other's faces, but when she's not they'll use it to try to see up the girls' skirts.

When it's their turn, the other girls will giggle.

Maybe you should giggle too. You all wear shorts under your skirts. The boys know that. But still, this feels so disgusting.

When it's your turn, the giggles won't come. You'll press your legs so far together you'll get bruises inside your knees and ankles and you'll wonder why you're suddenly so different.

CHAPTER 2

MOM HAS MADE CHICKEN BREAST WITH bruschetta topping, homemade pita chips, and a big green salad. She always cooks like we're at a four-star restaurant when Jeremy is here. Even on Fridays when we're supposed to be ordering pizza.

When I come out of my room, Mom is pulling out our four tray tables and arranging them in the living room, trying to make them look like a real dining room table. She still hasn't showered but I can smell that dinner is almost ready. She walks to the drawer where she keeps our linens and then looks up. She stares at me for a beat. I'm dressed in my baggy blue jeans and a long-sleeved white T-shirt with black dogs printed all over it.

"Lydia," she says, "aren't you hot?"

She says the same thing every day. I hate it.

I walk to the fake table and help her put on a lilac table-cloth so that it starts to look a little more real.

"Dinner smells good," I say. I want Mom to feel good about the good things. About letting me shower before her every day and about providing everything we need by being a lawyer and about being a really good cook.

"I hope it is." She glances at the clock above the stove. "Oh my goodness, he'll be here any minute," she says. "I have to rinse off."

As soon as she's gone, the buzzer buzzes. I look at the door to our room, where Emma is lounging on her bed listening to her iPod.

Come out. Come out, I think.

I don't want to open the door. Even though I shouldn't have a problem with Jeremy. I should love how Jeremy laughs all the time, so much that his belly shakes. How he makes jokes. How he fixes things in our apartment. How he makes Mom laugh.

I should know better than to look for signs of creepiness in my mom's boyfriend.

If there's one person I should trust more than anyone, it's my mom.

Still . . . if Emma answers the door it'll be better.

The buzzer buzzes again.

I go into our room, pull out the Stephen King novel I've been reading when Mom isn't looking, and flop onto my bed.

The buzzer buzzes.

"Aren't you going to get that?" Emma says.

"Aren't you?" I ask.

It buzzes again.

"What's wrong with you?" Emma says.

"Nothing," I say. "I just want to read."

I open my book.

The buzzer buzzes again.

"You know she'll be mad at you," Emma says. "She never gets mad at me."

That's true.

I put my book down and get up, walk to the buzzer beside our front door, and press the green button. "Hello?" I say.

Jeremy's big laugh comes crackling through the speaker. "Oh, sweetheart," he says. "I was worried no one was there. Let me up, will ya?"

I press the button that looks like a door. I unlock the front door to our apartment. Then I sit on the couch.

We live on the tenth floor, which means I have about five minutes.

"Lydia, my Lydia," he says as he opens the door. I am definitely not his Lydia. He's been dating my mom for only six months. I'm Dad's Lydia. I'm Mom's Lydia. I'm not his Lydia. "It's so good to see ya!"

He's been away for a week. That's not very long for me to go without seeing anyone who isn't my mom.

Jeremy is tall and big in all directions. Big head, big arms, big legs. Mom says he's jolly, like Santa. He is usually smiling and laughing all the time, but he sometimes looks at me in a way that feels very un-Santa.

He sits on the couch next to me and slides an arm behind my neck. He's wearing short sleeves, so our skin rubs together for the length of his arm. I think about the sweaty purple turtleneck in the laundry hamper. I wish I were still wearing it.

I stiffen.

Is this weird? Or is it just weird to me?

I wish Mom could see it. She'd react if it was weird. She'd let me know if it's just my brain working too hard.

"Tell me what you did today," he says.

"Just cleaned the house," I say.

Jeremy looks around. His arm wiggles on the back of my neck. I can feel his arm hair brushing against my jaw.

I should grow my hair long. Long enough that it can cover my neck and part of my face like a brown, shiny curtain. It'll be another layer of protection. My short, spiky haircut is doing nothing for me right now.

"This place?" he says. "Your mom always keeps it clean."

I freeze. Jeremy doesn't know about the house? Mom did not tell Jeremy, her boyfriend, about the house.

I stumble for a second. I don't like lying.

Emma bursts out of our room all sunshiny. "Jeremy!" she says. He gets up and gives her a bear hug. Her feet lift off the ground. I'm so relieved to have his arm away from my neck but still queasy watching him hug her like that.

But she hugs him back, giggling.

"You got anything for me?"

"You know I do!" he says.